Stories from the Shoe Store
Little Black Dress and Big Expectations

To Kimberly
Wishing you all love, laughter and a fabulous sense of style,
xx Emilija

To you, dear reader, for making this journey truly worthwhile.
And to Jil—I hope you grow to love reading.

'We tell ourselves stories in order to live. We interpret what we see, select the most workable of multiple choices. We live entirely, especially if we are writers, by the imposition of a narrative line upon disparate images, by the ideas with which we have learned to freeze the shifting phantasmagoria which is our actual experience.'

—JOAN DIDION, THE WHITE ALBUM

CHAPTER ONE

Before leaving the apartment, I stole a quick glance at my reflection in the hallway's grand mahogany mirror, channelling my inner Marie Antoinette. The rich wood warmed the space as I scrutinised my appearance. My usually straight brown hair was styled in loose, glossy waves that framed my face. Soft, earthy eyeshadow accentuated my eyes, and a sheer wash of rosy blush and nude lipstick softened my features.

As I met my own gaze, a surge of confidence and satisfaction swept over me. For this momentous occasion, I opted for my beloved little black Valentino—an exquisite blend of contemporary mastery echoing the timelessness of its silhouette. Crafted from the finest silk, the cool fabric glided over my hips, enveloping me in a cloud of sophistication. It felt like a gentle embrace from refinement itself, a reminder that I deserve nothing but the best in life. The off-shoulder neckline, a tribute to delicate craftsmanship, gracefully highlighted my collarbones, infusing the outfit with an extra layer of sensuality. This subtle yet intentional detail became a focal point, enhancing the dress's design with an understated yet captivating charm and sexiness. It artfully unveiled just enough, offering a teasing glimpse of skin without overshadowing the rest, achieving a perfect equilibrium between seduction and classiness. With every step, the dress seemed to come alive, catching the light just right, casting a glow that was part old Hollywood glamour, part modern-day magic.

Sixty years prior, in 1961, on Fifth Avenue, the most iconic little black dress in cinematic history graced the scene, emerging in front of the illustrious Tiffany's. Paired with pearls and collectively known as 'basic black', a ubiquitous trend of the early 1960s, the dress was accompanied by black evening gloves, a croissant, and a coffee—the latter two playfully lending an air of je ne sais quoi. Crafted by the visionary Givenchy, this black cocktail-style frock represented the epitome of a modern interpretation of the little black dress phenomenon. An intriguing detail often overlooked is that the original version of Givenchy's black dress was shorter than the one immortalised on screen, remaining unworn in the movie. This lesser-known fact adds a layer of mystery to the iconic garment.

My deliberate choice to forgo pearls signalled a nod to the evolving times, a conscious departure from the fashion norms of the 1960s. My era's 'basic black' was redefined through a slightly shorter and more fitted dress of the same colour, and delicate diamonds that caught the light gracefully with every subtle movement.

Ensuring I had all the essentials for the night ahead, I meticulously packed my Rouge Allure Velvet lipstick, credit card, and keys into one of my cherished vintage Serpenti clutches. That particular accessory had become more than just a stylish companion. Unintentionally, it had become a tradition for special occasions, almost as if it held a secret pact with the moments it witnessed—perhaps causing a hint of envy among the other handbags in my closet.

I practically tumbled down the stairs, two steps at a time, my trusty Saint Laurents keeping pace with my excitement. Forget Cinderella's glass slipper—these beauties hugged my feet like a good friend: comfy, stylish, and the perfect complement to my hard-earned tan. I still didn't know exactly where we were going, but my Nuits were coming along for the fabulous ride.

It's going to be a great night, I thought to myself.

The captivating story of the little black dress unfolds even before the fateful pairing of Audrey Hepburn and Givenchy. In 1926, American Vogue published a drawing of a simple black dress in crêpe de Chine. This calf-length, long-sleeved creation, embellished with a few diagonal lines and the quintessential string of pearls, earned the moniker 'Chanel's Ford' from Vogue. Much like Ford's Model T—the first affordable automobile for middle-class Americans—the little black dress epitomised effortlessness and accessibility, transcending social classes during its debut. Released amidst the financial hardships of the Great Depression, the dress spoke to the era's necessity for simplicity and affordability. As war rationing extended to textiles and fabrics, the LBD emerged unscathed, becoming the go-to choice for women back home. Vogue astutely predicted that it would evolve into 'a sort of uniform for all women of taste'. With its widespread adoption across classes, society grew accustomed to the sight of women dressed in black, radiating elegance without the burden of extravagance.

As a fashion staple, the little black dress has seen variations, often featuring velvet and lace for evening wear and wool for daytime attire. I personally owned a few different options. Among my favourites was also a turtleneck version, made from a deliciously comfortable and stretchy cotton fibre— a go-to choice for the chilly European months.

Notably, Wallis Simpson, the Duchess of Windsor, became synonymous with a stunning collection of little black dresses. Her famous proclamation, 'When a little black dress is right, there is nothing else to wear in its place,' captures the enduring glamour and versatility of this wardrobe essential. It is a sartorial chameleon, capable of adapting to various occasions with grace. Whether it graces the cocktail parties of high society or stands as a sophisticated choice for an intimate dinner, this particular staple has an uncanny ability to accentuate the wearer's individuality while embodying the aspiration of chic sophistication. The little black dress whispers a story of confidence, mystery, and enduring style, ensuring its perpetual reign as a symbol of femininity and sophistication.

...

Earlier that year. 2022.

The story went on. Life continued its relentless march forward. Unfortunately, so did global warming—a grim reality we'd later come to anticipate. Amidst it all, the only thing seemingly frozen in time was my watch. Every tick-tock felt like an eternity as I eagerly awaited our reunion. Just four more hours until time itself could halt. In that moment, the universe could cease its motion, and if I had my way, global warming would grind to a standstill, too.

When we talk about tackling global warming, it's clear that every decision counts. Sustainability is more than a buzzword; it's a lifestyle, a conscious effort to minimise our impact on the planet. Some people give up their seemingly comfortable lives as they know it in pursuit of 'going green'. While pondering the impending arrival of his plane may seem trivial in the grand scheme of things, it's important to acknowledge the broader implications of our choices. One such choice could have been to seek out a partner that lived in the same city, thereby reducing the need for frequent air travel and its associated carbon footprint. Lately, I have been struggling with that decision.

I try to reflect on the bright side sometimes instead of dwelling on our planet's existential threats every day. In that same vein, it is incredible how new love can spice up our lives. It injects excitement, sparking a fire in our eyes, a smile on our lips, and a radiant glow to our skin. Love has this uncanny ability to render our hair fuller, or at least that was the delightful illusion I saw in the mirror after a fun evening with him. Feeling good translated into looking good; love catalysed a truly fantastic feeling, one that elicited a sense of desire, empowerment, and creativity.

Love's impact on our souls, bodies, and overall appearance is nothing short of extraordinary. No fashion trend or makeup trick could rival the confidence and radiance that love bestows upon us. I recall encountering a headline emblazoned in bold letters, warning: 'Be careful before falling in love'. The article cautioned against the potential for reordering one's daily priorities to be in alignment with their beloved's and the risk of losing oneself in the process. Every addiction, I would add, comes with its own set of consequences. Yet, in the face of such warnings, love remained the singular craving that occupied my thoughts. I was ready to handle whatever repercussions might arise, for he offered the love and care I sought, and I reciprocated with nothing less.

He requested that I prepare his favourite Greek-style stuffed peppers and leek pie for our dinner together. To complement these dishes, I curated a selection of sides, including a vibrant Greek salad with crisp cucumbers, tomatoes, and the most authentic briny feta I could find at the market. Succulent pepperoni and green olives added a savoury touch to the spread. Excited to elevate a regular dining experience into an intimate affair, I accessorised the table with the warm glow of white candles, their flickering flames casting a soft, golden hue across the dining room. Our places at the table received a touch of sophistication via soft cloth napkins in a soothing light blue hue, perfectly complementing the roots of the Greek-inspired cuisine.

To further enhance the ambience, I turned to the musical charm of Julio Iglesias, a personal favourite artist of mine. While at his apartment, he typically favoured movie scores or piano music—genres that I also appreciated—but on this particular day, I was yearning for something more familiar and amorous.

Speaking of amorous, I slipped into a flowing grey silk maxi dress, its luxurious fabric effortlessly revealing more of my form than it concealed. I was allowing my hair to air-dry that evening. Bending forward, I ran a brush through the tresses as I flipped my head upside down. For a brief moment, I resembled a lion, with my hair cascading in wild waves, before standing upright, ready to face the world with an untamed poise. I smiled at myself in the mirror as I thought of Alessia's favourite catchphrase: 'Keep your inner lion alive'. She always encouraged Sophia and me to thrive and expand, rather than stay small and scared because of our own limiting beliefs.

Just then, I remembered I had forgotten to call Alessia back. As I reached for my mobile phone, there were missed calls and a message from him.
(Daniel) I missed the flight. And the next one is tomorrow morning. I have to miss you a few hours more now.

I called him immediately, and while I was on the line, I texted Alessia.
(Me) Hey, do you want to come over for dinner?

I called twice, but he didn't answer.
(Alessia) Sure, I can be there in less than an hour. Should I pick up Sophia?
(Me) I haven't talked to her. I don't know what she's up to.
(Alessia) I'll call her. See you in a bit.

I reclined on the plush carpet in my flowing silk dress, the same dress that would now go unappreciated by him this evening. I was captivated by the melodies swirling around me, and I immersed myself in the lyrics. Lost in the music, time seemed to elude me until the ringing of the phone abruptly summoned me back to reality, prompting me to rise from the floor. I hurried to see who was calling, hoping it was him announcing that he hopped on an earlier flight, but it wasn't.

'We're on our way. But, what happened? Weren't you supposed to meet Daniel tonight?' Sophia called from the passenger seat of Alessia's Mini.

'He... missed his flight?' I responded, but my voice wavered like a question. A question I could not ask him directly since he wasn't answering his phone.

'Oh. Okay? We'll be there in a minute', Alessia said and then hung up.

Exactly sixty seconds later, the girls burst into the apartment, their presence infusing the space with energy and palpable excitement. Sophia, her short blonde hair impeccably styled, made an entrance reminiscent of a bursting firework in a dazzling mini-skirted suit. The unexpected pop of orange, yellow, and gold lit up my neutral apartment like sparks in the night sky. A gilded chain anchored the hems, adding that unmistakable Chanel touch which paid equal attention to the rearview as it did to the front. Rounding off her look were pointed-toe yellow Blahniks, clicking against the floor with the confident strut of a woman who knows she's making a statement.

On the flip side, Alessia's presence seemed to effortlessly meld with the colour palette of my living room. Her tall, slender figure radiated grace in a floor-length, chocolate-brown slip dress. A glimpse of her tanned legs emerged with each fluid movement toward me. Opting for white sneakers, she balanced casual comfort with chic style. Her dark brown hair, styled in loose waves, added a layer of sophistication to the simplicity of the cotton dress. Alessia's choice of statement earrings subtly sparkled, catching the flickering candlelight.

From the moment they crossed the threshold, it was evident that the girls' mission was to lift my spirits. Sophia's gaze zeroed in on me, and Alessia appraised the meticulously arranged table, her eyes lighting up with delight.

'I'm almost grateful for his missed flight. Just look at this table; it's set perfectly for the three of us to have a girls' dinner party!' Alessia proclaimed, hurriedly taking a seat.

With flair, she revealed a magnum bottle of rosè wine from her bag, which she then flung onto a nearby chair. Who cares about hanging up your expensive tote bag when you've got a bottle of wine to open? In an instant, the atmosphere underwent a welcomed shift, turning what was initially set to be a lonely evening into an unexpected celebration of friendship.

'That is one big bottle!' Sophia exclaimed, lifting up the weighty magnum vessel with both hands. 'Thanks!'

Alessia swiftly intervened, her directness cutting through the moment. 'That ain't for you, friend. You are not the one who got ditched today. And she put in all this effort, making both the table and herself look absolutely scrumptious.' She directed her attention toward me, tossing a wink in my direction.

One must commend Alessia for her straightforwardness. Also, with her bold vocabulary, one might easily mistake her for the frontwoman of a rap band. Yet, in the presence of her patients and medical colleagues, Alessia assumed a level of distinct and measured professionalism. Her ability to adapt her communication style depending on the context showcased her intelligence and charisma. Alessia, truly a force to be reckoned with, navigated different facets of life with finesse.

'And that is one big bag!' I couldn't help but notice the Chanel sitting beside Alessia. I pulled a chair for Sophia on the opposite side and sat next to her. Then I poured us some rosè from a slightly smaller bottle which I had already opened. My bottle had a portrait of Cleopatra on it.

'That isn't Cleopatra. It's just some random girl with an extravagant hair accessory. She's sitting at a bar, most probably in France, not in a pyramid in Egypt,' Alessia astutely observed.

'Let's be real here. Cleopatra had nothing to do with the pyramids. Those majestic structures were standing tall 2,000 years before she even set foot in this world.' Sophia always made an effort to be accurate when it came to historical facts.

'Cleopatra has absolutely nothing to do with this rosè, either. This bottle hails from the year 2021, a good 2,000 years after Cleopatra bid adieu to this world,' I chimed in, grateful to the girls for steering my thoughts away from Daniel's missed flight and into the realm of the Middle East.

The ancient Egyptians were the first civilisation to prioritise style over practicality, earning them an esteemed position in this book and any discourse on fashion history. Their profound fascination with the human body led them to craft clothing that seamlessly blended flattering aesthetics and practical functionality. In the complex story of ancient Egyptian civilisation, fashion surfaced as a powerful tool for expressing cultural identity, social status, and individual personality.
Cleopatra stands out as a timeless fashion icon of her era, her distinctive style a symbol to her infamous flair. Characterised by extravagant makeup and lavish jewellery, her look exuded an unmistakable uniqueness. Beyond the well-known ritual of her milk and honey baths, Cleopatra utilised a diverse array of rocks, plants, and minerals for her makeup regimen.

The effort she dedicated to her appearance shines through in these meticulous details of her beauty routine. Black kohl took on the dual role of both mascara and eyeliner, while red ochre graced her lips and cheeks to achieve a natural flush. With its rich pigments, Henna added a rich hue to her fingernails, serving as a precursor to contemporary nail polish.
Despite the seemingly laborious process, Cleopatra's dedication to makeup and jewellery remained unwavering. Her fondness for finery extended to massive gold headdresses embellished with sun disks, elaborate broad collars and serpent-inspired armbands. For Cleopatra, more was undoubtedly more, showcasing her genuine love for the artistry of cosmetics and the transformative appeal of exquisite accessorisation.

Although Cleopatra didn't necessarily invent any new styles, she utilised existing ones to her advantage. It's challenging to contemplate how she would feel knowing that her iconic look is predominantly used for costume parties nowadays. However, we should acknowledge her for her talent in transforming a simple white linen dress into a glamorous outfit and her ingenuity with makeup, something that might come in handy when our favourite Diorshow eyeshadows are out of stock.

She has been an inspiration to fashion and makeup enthusiasts worldwide, setting aside the aforementioned costume parties, leaving an avant-garde mark on fashion history as we know it. In preparation for the glamourous Cleopatra movie, the costume designer created sixty-five dresses, taking inspiration from a few Egyptian bas-reliefs, tomb paintings, and two available sculptures. However, it is difficult to determine the historical accuracy of Cleopatra's costumes since there is no clear record of how she dressed or what she even looked like. Although she was the queen of Egypt and lived in an Egyptian-style palace, she was actually Greek and probably wore Greek clothing most of the time. Only on ceremonial occasions would she have worn traditional ancient Egyptian clothing.

The costume designer didn't stick to the traditional Egyptian costume. She made this decision for two main reasons. Firstly, linen, which is the fabric traditionally used for Egyptian costumes, tends to wrinkle easily. As the costumes would need to be worn multiple times while repeating the scenes, the designer understandably chose to use a different material for practical reasons.

Secondly, having sixty-five white linen costumes would have been quite dull, regardless of how many karats of gold were added to them. One more thought on the movie: Cleopatra's appearance was quite different from Elizabeth Taylor's portrayal of her. She was not a conventional beauty, as evidenced by a small coin in the Society of Antiquaries of Newcastle collection, which was discovered in February of 2007. That coin presented a contrast to romanticised portrayals of Cleopatra. Roman writers praised her charisma, intelligence, and seductive voice but notably omitted any mention of her beauty. Despite not being conventionally beautiful, she was still an intriguing and captivating woman. It is worth noting that a woman's beauty isn't determined by her physical appearance alone. After Elizabeth Taylor's portrayal of her, it's difficult to imagine that Cleopatra had dark skin. However, in a more recent film that focused on her character rather than her clothing, an African actress played the role.

Back to our table. Two notable observations: Firstly, Cleopatra's wine of choice was Greek Muscat, not Provence rosé. Secondly, it wasn't Cleopatra's face gracing the label of our rosé that evening.

'It smells amazing! I love it when you bake. You're definitely my number one friend when it comes to making delicious pies!' Sophia exclaimed.

'Do you really believe you have any other friend who bakes?' Alessia teased.

'Hmm. No,' Sophia replied between bites. 'But back to the person this pie was baked for. What happened with his flight?' She redirected the conversation and my thoughts, switching her attention once again from Cleopatra to my culinary skills to the intriguing story behind the missed flight.

'I don't know any details,' I confessed, the uncertainty palpable in my voice. 'He caught my voicemail and left a brief message. I returned the call, but he didn't pick up.'

'It's not uncommon for him to dodge your calls, is it?' Alessia, her brow furrowed, questioned me. To tell the truth, she was accurate in her observation, but it never bothered me much.

Trying to steer away from the weighty topic again, Sophia interjected, 'Is he still planning to visit you for the weekend, at least?'

'Yes, tomorrow morning with the next flight, he wrote,' I replied, my uncertainty now undeniably audible, as if the words themselves betrayed a hint of doubt.

Alessia was perceptive, as always. 'Did you check online to see if there were any flights later this evening?'

'No, I didn't,' I admitted, briefly contemplating the idea before dismissing it. It felt too early in the relationship to start probing and questioning his actions.

As my gaze shifted between Sophia and Alessia, a knowing look passed between them. Sophia, radiating scepticism about my dating choices, and Alessia, adopting a cheerleader's attitude, declared with a playful grin, 'Well, at least you're giving the guy a chance. You do your best. Not everyone can be a dating expert.' Her reassurance was accompanied by a ripple of contagious laughter, injecting a light-hearted moment into the room and momentarily easing the tension.

'Are you saying you believe he's not the one?' I asked my friend.

'The one for what?' Alessia chuckled. 'The one to have some fun with until it maybe gets serious? Yeah, he is. The one to worry about what he's doing when he's not with you? No, he isn't. At least, not yet,' she concluded, offering her honest perspective on my budding relationship.

Alessia and Sophia were like two parallel universes, both uniquely captivating, yet together forming the cosmos of my social existence. I often found myself pondering the alternate reality where their vibrant personalities were not intertwined with my life. Their unwavering support and uplifting presence made a profound impact on me, an impact that I did not take for granted.

In the metaphorical seascape of life, Sophia embodied the serene beauty of a sandy coast, her warmth and tranquillity grounding me in moments of calm. On the other hand, scrappy and steadfast Alessia was the rocky coast, weathered by life's many storms yet still standing tall and unyielding.

Their lives had ventured into new chapters since the last time you, dear reader, met them in my first story. Sophia had been keeping herself busy with work. Well, I guess that hasn't really changed. She and Maurice, Martha's son, remained on good terms after they cleared the air, but it also became obvious that they wouldn't have any other shared passion than that of designer furniture. The suggestion of co-parenting lingered, a concept Maurice put forth, but Sophia, as practical as she might have been, still found the idea too unconventional. The intricacies of planning for a child in such a pragmatic manner felt awkward, which led her to gracefully step away from that path. Conversely, Alessia, ever the advocate, supported the notion wholeheartedly. 'Isn't this what you desired? A baby,' she would encourage Sophia, keenly aware of her friend's aspirations. 'I never heard you say you wanted to marry. Or even that you loved Maurice.'

Yet, Sophia's unspoken desires hinted at a longing for a family, not just a child. The complexity of her emotions danced between the prospect of contractual co-parenthood and the unforeseen possibility of true love making an unexpected entrance into her life.

Sophia knew Maurice was suitable for fathering her child, but the question lingered like a gentle breeze: what if true love suddenly appeared?

'Life's too short. Don't ponder "what if". Act on desires,' Alessia said. I nodded, realising the profound simplicity in those words.

The intricacies of Sophia's situation seemed numerous, each aspect urging attention, yet all of it seemed to lose its significance in the face of that resounding declaration: 'Life's too short.'

In the grand scheme of existence, the brevity of life begged to be acknowledged, urging a departure from the paralysis of 'what if' scenarios. Alessia's counsel became a beacon, guiding me to a space where the urgency of living eclipsed the minutiae of contemplation. The essence of her advice lingered, rendering everything else secondary compared to the truth encapsulated in those four words. Life is too short.
Alessia had mastered the art de vivre, her best life, and seized the present moment each day. She was an inspiration, a role model whose vibrant approach urged us to savour every day. I found myself gazing up to her as a role model, attempting to glean the secrets of her philosophy. But it wasn't merely about mirroring her actions. Alessia's ability to be fully present and relish life was an inherent facet of her character, an authenticity not easily duplicated. While Sophia and I acknowledged our shortcomings in this regard, we recognised the undeniable truth that Alessia was onto something, and we aspired to emulate her in our own ways.

Alessia had also been working on something monumental. It was a venture far more significant than a silly missed flight, and held a promise more tangible than the current state of my relationship. She was building a pathway to manifest all her dreams, aspirations, and wishes. In contrast to waiting for the right moment or relying on external forces, Alessia took charge. She was making things happen. As her best friends and supporters, we found ourselves caught up in the whirlwind of her ambition, eagerly anticipating our roles in this extraordinary new chapter of her life. This chapter loomed large, brimming with potential and excitement. Together, we were set to embark on a journey that held the potential of not only reshaping Alessia's life, but enriching ours as well.

That evening, amidst shared laughter and the clinking of glasses, Sophia confessed her desire to embody Alessia's uninhibited zest for life. Whether it was after the third or fourth glass, I can't remember, but suddenly, Sophia's words spilt out. 'I wish I was more like you,' she confessed to Alessia. 'You just live. Life happens to you because you let it. You genuinely mean yes when you say yes, and you say no when you want to say no. As for me, even when I know what I want, I get caught up thinking about what I should say. Then, it spirals into pondering what the other person expects me to say... and what the rest of the world wants me to say. And the world is vast. Do you know how long it takes until I decide what the rest of the world would want me to say?' Sophia concluded her heartfelt monologue, slightly out of breath, and then, the tension dissolved into shared laughter.

We all joined in, and Alessia—standing up from her chair—enveloped Sophia in a tight hug, a sweet gesture of understanding and friendship that spoke volumes without the need for words.

'You're incredible, and I genuinely mean it,' Alessia said, her eyes sparkling with sincerity. 'You're my only friend who knows that Cleopatra and Mark Antony formed their drinking club in 40 B.C. I've learned so much from you, and not just factoids but genuinely useful knowledge. I'd be thrilled if there was anything I could contribute that you find valuable, too.'

As the voices of my two wise friends filled the air, a nagging question surfaced within me: can the art of living in the present moment be learned, or is it an inherent aspect of one's personality, a trait ingrained from birth? Though I didn't have all the answers, I felt compelled to embark on a journey to find them. I vowed to myself, a silent promise echoing in the recesses of my mind, that I would embrace the present henceforth. Will I see him tomorrow? I had my wonderful friends with me at that moment, and we were enjoying a delicious dinner, good wine, and quality time with each other, which was a rare commodity of late. We had everything to relish in the present, almost nothing to regret about the past, and the future was filled with promises. So, I chose to discard that question far, far away from my mind.

It wasn't until the next day unfolded that I heard from him—his voice reaching out from the confines of a taxi, a telephonic connection spanning the distance and bridging the gap between our worlds.

'I'm en route to the airport,' his cheerful voice took over, the background noise of traffic faintly audible. 'See you shortly. How about we meet at your place and head somewhere nice for breakfast?'

'Safe travels. Let's stay in. I'll prepare breakfast for us.'

Opting to savour the moment, I resisted the urge to delve into why he hadn't returned my call the day before. I had pledged to live in the present, and on that very day, I made a conscious decision to embrace the now. Focusing on the happiness of seeing him soon, I let go of the rest, recognising its diminished significance, if any at all.

CHAPTER TWO

The mystery of whether Martha was aware of the brief romance between Sophia and her son remained unsolved. He may have confided in her, but perhaps the memory had slipped through the cracks of time. Alternatively, Martha might have deemed it inappropriate to discuss such matters with me. Regardless, her demeanour reflected a woman in good spirits, eagerly anticipating an upcoming trip to one of her favourite cities—a city that was coincidentally dear to my heart as well. Venice beckoned, and I, too, was counting down the days until my own visit the following weekend.

'If I had known you were also headed there, I would have delayed my plans and made it a joint girls' trip,' Martha exclaimed, her words delivered with a familiar warmth. Her dark green eyes sparkled with vitality, an arresting feature that highlighted both her wisdom and an ever-youthful zest for life. A perpetual smile graced her face, complementing the soft rose-toned lipstick she wore every single day since I've known her. Despite eschewing the use of highlighter, Martha's skin emanated a natural glow, a reflection of the inner vibrancy that required no artificial enhancement. Her hair, gracefully and naturally white, had a soft sheen to it. It was almost always tucked away in a flowy French twist. Though her figure had become petite with the passage of years, glimpses of her former figure shone through. Martha's upright and elegant posture hinted at a past dedication to maintaining a healthy physique. When I was in her presence, I felt like a student attending a masterclass in effortless charm. She left an undeniable impression on those fortunate enough to know her. As a customer in the shoe store, she brought with her not only an appreciation for fashion, but also an enduring grace that elevated the ambience of the space. Other customers in the store benefitted from her presence, considering she was never too shy to share her opinions on trends, old and new.

On that particular day, Martha wasn't on a quest for new additions to her already extensive collection of shoes. Recognising the opportunity to offer her a momentary break from her daily responsibilities of tending to Madame and Gigi, I extended a warm invitation for a glass of champagne, ensuring Madame had her own bowl of water—a gesture I always found charming when furry friends came into the shop.

Comfortably settled in the inviting red velvet armchair near the cash register, Martha shared her excitement about travelling to Venice. Her recent lack of travel made the anticipation of this upcoming adventure particularly delightful. As she spoke, her eyes widened with joy, radiating enthusiasm for a topic that brought her immense pleasure at this stage of life.

In my opinion, Martha had lived a life that approached perfection. Although she hadn't pursued a conventional career, she found fulfilment in the refined hobbies she cherished—painting, collecting art, reading, and actively participating in the organisation of charities for her late husband's company. Her home had become a hub for elegant gatherings, parties, and events.

After her husband's passing, Martha's focus shifted. Her eyes now sparkled most brightly when the conversation turned to travel, her furry companions, and, of course, shoes. In these endeavours, Martha discovered ongoing joy and fulfilment, creating a new life that blended sophistication with heartfelt joy in her golden years.

Her kind offer to visit Venice together resonated deeply as I pondered our relationship, realising that, despite the warmth and familiarity, we weren't truly friends. She was, after all, a customer—a cherished one, but a customer nonetheless. I realised then that my heart yearned for the companionship of Sophia and Alessia on this Venetian adventure. Alas, Alessia's schedule couldn't accommodate the trip that weekend, and Venice Fashion Week, with its own bustling agenda, waited for no one.

'An Italian vacation with you would have been delightful,' I responded, adding, 'Considering you're a regular visitor, I'm sure you've uncovered many hidden gems in that city.'

'Oh, absolutely! You simply can't miss the Wiener schnitzel at Harry's Bar. I know it's a traditional Austrian dish, but at Harry's, they prepare it so tender and crispy it could almost make you forget about pasta. The Bellini cocktail, too. It's a delicious blend of peach puree and Prosecco, invented by the founder of Harry's Bar, Giuseppe Cipriani. But what really sets Harry's Bar apart are the views—I mean, how could anyone complain when they're looking out at the stunning Venetian lagoon.' Martha recommended this establishment with such vigour I almost felt like I was there at Harry's with her.

The notion of enjoying a schnitzel in Venice, or even Italy, struck me as unconventional but intriguing. It was probably an enticing suggestion for a devoted schnitzel enthusiast. I would be more like, - the schnitzel menu, please, but for me, only the French fries. And the Bellini cocktail with a view.

Martha had orchestrated her journey to Venice a week before Sophia and I had planned to go, where we would be accompanied by a friend from Paris whom she had connected with during one of her sojourns in Rome. Their shared love for Italy, profound appreciation for its rich culture, passion for authentic made-in-Italy products, and elevated tastes in hotels and restaurants knit them together. Yet, beneath their shared enthusiasm for Italy, I sensed a shared experience of lives marked by solitude.

The idea of sharing solitude with someone holds a unique appeal—the idea that when solitude is shared, its weight becomes lighter and less burdensome. It speaks to the truth that companionship has the power to alleviate the sometimes isolating aspects of one's journey through life. The prospect of experiencing solitude alongside a kindred spirit transforms it into a shared, more manageable hardship.

Shortly after her departure, an unexpected visitor graced the store—none other than Sophia.

'You just missed Maurice's mum,' I informed Sophia, a note of uncertainty threading through my words, not quite certain of what response I was about to get.

'Has she shared anything with you?' Sophia inquired, her expression guarded, attempting to maintain a poker face that betrayed little of her inner thoughts.

'No. I'm unsure if Martha is aware of anything at all,' I responded.

'That might be for the best. By the way, was she the lady with the dark blue Chanels and the light blue Brunello Cucinelli coat? The golden retriever and the cocker spaniel, both sporting the cutest Tiffany collars?' Sophia's keen eye for detail was unmistakable.

I nodded, wondering if she could also vividly describe the multitude of individuals she encountered on the street while en route to the boutique.

'We crossed paths. I admired her style. The dogs were adorable. A smile passed between us. Think about it: today, I could have been strolling with those dogs alongside her,' Sophia mused. She seemed on the brink of expressing more but opted for brevity, concluding with, 'She looked like a very fine lady.'

'You look like a very fine lady, too.' I embraced the delicate cashmere scarf around her neck, inhaling the soothing fragrance of her perfume. Sophia pivoted to reveal her latest acquisition: a cashmere coat, just a shade lighter than Martha's dog's fur, with a thick belt in the same hue defining her waist. I envisioned how a blue Tiffany collar could have complemented the outfit if it were available as a belt for humans. It sparked a whimsical thought about whether they manufactured such accessories only for dogs.

'I'm treating you to lunch. Come, slip on your coat.' Sophia said with a mischievous glimmer in her eye.

I hastened, mildly astonished at the rare spectacle unfolding before me. Sophia taking a break from work for lunch?

Once in a blue moon.

While heading towards the bistro, we meandered past the Tiffany's storefront. As we peered through the window, our eyes were drawn towards the exquisite display of those eccentric blue pet collars.

Tiffany Blue stands as a brand colour renowned for its iconic and emotional resonance. This particular shade possesses a captivating ability to evoke feelings of joy and wonder in those fortunate enough to encounter it—including myself. Since 1845, Tiffany & Co. has proudly identified itself with this distinctive colour. This legacy began with the introduction of its first Blue Book catalogue, featuring a cover bathed in the now-famous shade that is now referred to as 'Tiffany Blue'. This colour, often described as 'forget-me-not' blue or 'robin's egg' blue, was intentionally chosen due to the prevailing popularity of turquoise gemstones during the 19th century.

Turquoise held a special place in the hearts of Victorian brides, who often gifted dove-shaped brooches set with turquoise to their attendants as a keepsake, personifying the true sentiment of 'forget-me-not' blue. The familiar wedding adage, 'Something old, something new, something borrowed, and something blue', echoes this tradition. In the Victorian era, blue symbolises love, purity, and fidelity—three virtues considered indispensable for a resilient and enduring marriage. Wearing or carrying something blue was also believed to ward off the Evil Eye, adding an element of superstition to the symbolism. Charles Lewis Tiffany, the visionary behind the brand's ascent to the pinnacle of wedding luxury, embraced these traditions. After selecting a specific shade of blue, he entrenched it as the signature colour of the Tiffany & Co. brand, aligning it with the profound and timeless qualities associated with love and matrimony.

A century later, the iconic 'little blue box' has evolved into a symbol of lavishness, continuing to embody enduring love. In my personal quest for the perfect gift on two separate occasions, I embarked on a journey to Tiffany & Co., captivated by the appeal of finding something extraordinary for someone dear during significant milestones. A remarkable observation struck me on both visits: the 'little blue box' was never offered for seemingly personal indulgence. This charming detail added an extra layer of sentimentality to the already unique experience of gifting from Tiffany's.

'I'll always love Tiffany Blue. However, they lost me at their latest collection of chunky chains. It's just not the same Tiffany or Audrey Hepburn vibe,' Sophia remarked, her disappointment evident.

I glanced at the oversized chains on display, each link telling a completely different story than the delicate pieces that once graced the iconic brand.

'I suppose those chains still possess a certain femininity,' I interjected, attempting to find a redeeming quality.

Sophia sighed, her discerning eyes studying the display. 'I don't hate them. It just feels more Versace than the quintessential Tiffany aesthetic we've come to love.'

'It's alright. I can't afford them anyway,' I added with a wink.

Her face lit up. 'Not yet, at least. Maybe you'll become rich and famous soon.'

En route to lunch, Sophia, amidst sharing her candid thoughts on the latest Tiffany collection, began to unveil some thrilling plans that instantly captured my attention.

'I'm contemplating writing a captivating story for the magazine about our upcoming trip to Venice. Picture this: a fashion weekend in Venice featuring both models, and non-models like yourself. I've arranged for a photographer to accompany us, capturing incredible shots against the stunning backdrop of the Canale Grande, with you dressed in haute couture.' Sophia shared, her eyes sparkled as the words continued falling out of her mouth like an avalanche.

'Me? As a model in a magazine?' I asked, a mix of surprise and curiosity in my voice.

'As someone outside the realm of professional modelling,' Sophia clarified with a laughter-laced statement, emphasising the inclusivity of the envisioned project.

'What should I wear?' I inquired, already dreaming up the possibilities.

'We'll curate a selection from the latest collections. It's an excellent opportunity for the boutique's marketing as well. We can highlight that you work at the store. And the best part—I'm extending an invitation, so you won't have to worry about covering the cost of that luxurious hotel at the Grand Canal you had your eye on,' Sophia explained, carefully unveiling the most enticing of details.

'That's quite tempting,' I admitted.

'So?' Sophia pressed, awaiting my decision.

'I'm in. A non-model model.' Sophia knew she had me hooked. Being a good friend, I couldn't resist the opportunity to support her, especially as she navigated through the complexities of her recent unlucky love story. Besides, the magazine boasted an impressive wardrobe collection. I was not going to turn down an opportunity to play dress-up.

    And with that, Sophia had basically packed my luggage for me, and also covered the expenses for my room, flight, and water taxi. She had thought of everything, and all I needed to do was show up. I felt like a star. Like a non-star star.

CHAPTER THREE

When I think of Venice, it's not just the canals or the gondolas that come to mind. No, it's a different shade of blue entirely. Venetian Blue—a colour so rich, so captivating, it's as if the city itself took a brush and painted my imagination. A resolute hue resembling cobalt, it carries with it the mystique of legend. As the story goes, this colour found its way to Venice through enigmatic cargo, arriving via the city's maritime trade routes from the East. It was this vibrant trade that rendered the kingdom of the Doge the pioneer in Europe to embrace previously unseen fabrics, brocades, and hues. Among these treasures, Venetian Blue stood out, swiftly sweeping the continent. Yet, in a nod to its origins, the colour retained its name, a reflection of its authentic Venetian heritage.

And isn't that just like life? We collect experiences—some foreign, some familiar—and they become a part of us. Like the Venetian Blue that once traveled miles from the East to Venice, we pick up pieces of the world and weave them into our own stories. But no matter how far we go, some things never lose their original essence, forever holding onto the places they first called home.

When we touched down in Venice, our laughter echoed through the baggage carousel as Sophia quipped about, audibly praying the water taxi wouldn't succumb to the weight of our luggage. We walked toward the exit, and amidst the lively banter, our eyes swiftly caught our driver, who was standing at the arrivals gate proudly displaying our surnames on a board in large, bold letters. It was a charming touch that paid homage to the Italians' inherent casualness, where titles like Ms. or Mrs. and the formality of family names were replaced with a warm and straightforward embrace of simplicity.

Venice was perpetually humming with vitality. A dynamic hub, it welcomed many events—from the prestigious Biennale and film festivals to captivating art exhibitions and the appeal of fashion weeks. And, if ever there was a lull, the city's timeless charm played host to romantic weddings, ensuring its streets were perennially graced with the buzz of activity and the celebration of love.

For centuries, Venice held the esteemed title of the fashion capital. Its unique style broke free from standardised rules, instead charting its course fueled by emotion. In this captivating city, women dressed themselves freely, showcasing the emergence of liberated expression. Venetian women, both aristocrats and libertines, curated distinctive styles that set them apart not only from the rest of Italy but also from the entire European landscape.

While women in other cities adhered to stringent dress codes dictated by harsh regulations that mandated high-necked styles, the women of Venice revelled in a sense of control over their appearance. Defying the conventions imposed by the Church of Rome, Venice embraced a religious independence distinct from the prevailing Catholicism of the era. This autonomy extended beyond matters of faith, granting the people of Venice remarkable freedom in shaping their styles and clothing, a freedom seldom witnessed elsewhere. As such, the city became a monumental haven where individuals could unabashedly express themselves, unencumbered by the religious norms that prevailed in other corners of the world.

In the whirlwind world of Venetian fashion, daring dresses always had their trusty sidekicks: the iconic *calcagnini* or *coping*, revered as the ultimate luxurious footwear reserved solely for the elite of Venice. With their thick soles, these predecessors of today's wedges didn't just add height; they sculpted the wearer's silhouette to perfection. But what's a show-stopping look without a touch of sparkle? Jewels were the pièce de résistance, adding that extra dash of extravagance. And let's not forget the fan—a must-have accessory that added a hint of intrigue, skillfully concealing a smile or evading direct eye contact with a suitor.

Arguably, even more emblematic of Venice than the fan and Venetian Blue is the Burano lace. Its origins are steeped in romance, tracing back to an ancient fisherman engaged to a captivating girl on the island. Legend has it that, as on many days before, he set out to fish in the East Sea lagoon. To his surprise, mesmerising sirens surrounded him, attempting to lure him with their melodious voices. The young man, guided by an unwavering love for his fiancée, resisted the temptation (bearing in mind that it is a legend). Impressed by his faithfulness, the sirens' queen bestowed a gift upon him: she struck the side of the boat with her tail, creating a foam that transformed into a breathtaking wedding veil. Upon returning home, the fisherman presented the unique piece to his fiancée. Admired and envied by the island's young ladies, they began imitating the lace of the wedding veil, employing increasingly finer needle-and-thread, aspiring to craft even more exquisite lace for their own wedding dresses.

The true origin of Burano lace, while less fantastical than the legend, still carries a charm that is almost as romantic. Inhabitants of the island, primarily fishermen and their industrious wives, often found themselves mending the men's fishing nets using basic needles and sturdy thread. Yet, as they awaited the return of their husbands for hours, these resourceful women transitioned to finer needles and higher-quality threads, transforming the mundane task into an artistic, refined, and creative endeavour. Remarkably, they crafted intricate lace pieces using only a needle and thread, entirely without any cloth support. And thus, the exquisite tradition of lace-making was born on the charming island of Burano.

Fast-forward to a starlit night in Venice, where Burano stepped into the spotlight once more. Here, in a dazzling display of contemporary artistry, the island's legacy met the cutting-edge vision of the time. Atelier Martina Vidal and the visionary designer Michela Gaiofatto collaborated to unveil a breathtaking collection. The garments that graced the catwalk were nothing short of romantic, embodying a sense of purity and feminine charm. I couldn't help but imagine the sumptuous textures caressing the models' skin, a reflection of the impressive craftsmanship that defined each piece.

Atelier Martina Vidal, led by the visionary duo Martina and Sergio Vidal, represented the fourth generation committed to preserving the rich legacy of Burano lace. Their dedication to the traditional techniques passed down through generations was evident in every delicate stitch and intricate pattern. Yet, their creativity knew no bounds as they propelled the revered craft into the future, exploring new forms and designs that breathed fresh life into the tiny island of Burano.

The following morning, as the sun brushed the sky over Venice with strokes of gold and rose, Sophia and I embarked on the journey to Burano Island itself, understandably referred to as the Lace Island. The moment we set foot on its cobblestone streets, we were met with a vibrant spectacle—a colourful array of houses that painted the landscape like a masterpiece in motion. Each building boasted its own unique hue, forming a mosaic that stretched the limits of imagination. It was as if we had stepped into the pages of a whimsical children's book, where every corner held the promise of a delightful adventure.

The streets of Burano were alive with the rhythmic dance of laundry swaying gently in the breeze. Clotheslines crisscrossed above us, draped with garments in an array of colours, casting playful shadows on the sunlit pathways. It was as if the island itself had woven a magical spell, transforming everyday scenes into a spectacle of artistry for all to behold. Looking into the windows of the charming boutiques, skilled artisans meticulously crafted the well-known and intricate lace patterns, their hands moving with a grace that mirrored the island's grace.

I was thrilled to have the opportunity to witness the creative lace-making process and observe both the contemporary and well-preserved antique samples. Engaging in conversations with the local lacemakers was a genuine pleasure. While my Italian might not have been as fluent as a native's, it proved sufficient for exchanging compliments and laughter. Sophia, ever the diligent journalist, reminded me to take detailed notes, emphasising the importance of capturing the essence of this ancient craft for her upcoming article. I was actually asking one lady for a restaurant recommendation then, but I nodded in agreement to please my generous benefactor who had orchestrated this once-in-a-lifetime experience.

In the cosy ambience of a traditional Burano tavern situated at Piazza Galuppi, we indulged in the obligatory risotto de gò. The dish, prepared with a flavorful broth made from fish caught in the local lagoon, was a culinary ode to the marine treasures that surrounded the charming Lace Island.

Satiated with the delectable flavours of the sea, we reluctantly bid adieu to the many delights of Burano. We had to embark on a journey across the lagoon, past Burano Island, to the Grand Canal, where our hotel awaited. I promised Sophia to pose for photos, and she promised to join me at the Peggy Guggenheim Gallery, where art and culture would weave another layer into our Venetian adventure.

'Taxi!' Sophia's voice rang, her call slicing through the air as she swiftly hailed one amidst the empty dock.

'Where to?' Inquired the handsome driver, exuding a confident charm that conveyed he was ready to whisk us away from our Burano adventure.

'To Hotel Baglioni, please,' Sophia said.

'At your service,' he responded with a huge smile, revealing perfectly positioned teeth that added to the charismatic aura surrounding him.

The handsome Italian gentleman, oozing charm like the sun on a summer day, kindly helped us onto the boat. He sported a crisp white linen shirt, perfectly complementing his bronzed skin. Those white shorts with funky black dots? Talk about playful elegance! They hugged his toned physique, hinting at a laid-back yet sophisticated vibe.

Is this your first visit to Venice?' he asked Sophia, and I couldn't help but notice that his English was perfect—too perfect. Not even a hint of the charming Italian accent I'd secretly been hoping for. But I had to admit, accent or no accent, he was still undeniably charming. And he looked good. Sophia noticed that too; I knew that if he didn't look so good, she wouldn't have spent the entire drive talking to a stranger instead of obsessively checking her work emails.

Under the midday sun's warm embrace, we navigated the intricate water passages of Venice, bidding our final farewell to the picturesque Lace Island. The water taxi gracefully carried us through the labyrinthine canals, and I was breathing in all the sights, sounds, and smells. As we approached Venice, majestic palazzos adorned with intricate architectural details emerged, their pastel facades casting gentle reflections upon the glistening waters below. We passed beneath the elegant arches of the Rialto Bridge, each turn revealing yet another facet of Venice's timeless beauty. Meanwhile, Sophia remained immersed in conversation with our chatty driver, seemingly unfazed by the captivating scenery unfolding around us.

Upon reaching our designated stop, the driver surprised us by refusing payment. Sophia, determined to settle the fare, engaged in a friendly banter with him. To our amusement, he boldly claimed he wasn't even a taxi driver.

'Why did you think I was a taxi driver in the first place?' he inquired.

'Is this not your boat?' Sophia retorted with a question, her tone serious as usual, her eyes locked onto his.

'It is. I mean, it belongs to a friend, but he's not a taxi driver either. What about this boat says "taxi"?' We examined the sleek wooden motorboat with its retro design and modern, snow-white interior. It was a good question, indeed. The absence of a logo or any mention of 'taxi' left us scratching our heads.

Sophia, undeterred, continued her questioning. 'Why did you take us then?'

'Because I liked you,' he replied nonchalantly, as if offering rides to people he liked was an absolute no-brainer. When you see someone you like, you offer them a ride and use that precious time to talk to them. If possible, you take the longer route. I was contemplating in my head, my thoughts waving around the unconventional scenario. We were the ones who initiated the ride, but he embraced the opportunity for conversation.

So, is this your daily routine? Taking girls you like for a ride and charming the pants off them? You really have that much free time on your hands?' Sophia was being sassy. I recognized that blend of annoyance and curiosity all too well.

'Yep, I've got plenty of free time,' he said, flashing that gorgeous smile again. 'Truth is, I'm pretty busy, just like everyone else here in Venice, rushing around to see as much as they can without really taking the time to feel the city. Today, your stop just happened to be on my route. However, I do have some extra time tonight around ten, in case you need a ride.' His offer wasn't exactly straight out of a gentleman's playbook, but there was a playful charm to it that I could tell Sophia wasn't immune to. As he helped us out of the Water Cabrio, he placed a polite kiss on the back of our hands—Sophia's, with a hint of affection; mine, purely out of courtesy. But what really caught me off guard? Sophia, handing him her phone for a contact exchange.

'That was the first Italian I've heard speaking perfect British English,' I commented to Sophia as the motor roared to life behind us.

'How do you know he was even Italian? He wasn't even a taxi driver. We don't know anything about him,' Sophia raised a valid point. And that only made him more intriguing. Laughter bubbled up between us, as our romance film-adjacent encounter became an unexpected twist in our Venetian adventure.

'Hmm. What was his name?' I inquired, a subtle curiosity lacing my words.

'I don't know,' Sophia replied nonchalantly.

'You didn't ask for his name? What did you talk about the whole time?'

'Why should I have asked the taxi driver for his name?' Sophia tried to dismiss her interest like she always did.

'He wasn't a taxi driver,' I reminded her.

'Hmm,' she responded ambiguously, her thoughts veiled behind the noncommittal sound.

'I mean, he gave you his phone number. Under which name did he save it?' I pressed on, genuinely curious myself.

Sophia looked down at her phone, chuckled, and looked back up at me. 'Taxi!' We burst into hearty laughter, tears streaming down our faces as we clung to each other, wheezing. The surrounding onlookers turned their heads, sharing a giggle. To them, we must have seemed intoxicated. Nothing was as it seemed in Venice. Not even the taxis.

A compelling anecdote comes to mind when thinking about appearances being deceiving, and although it doesn't have any connection to Venice, it's worth sharing. Upon the launch of her inaugural issue of American Vogue, Anna Wintour made a notable decision. The cover featured a photograph by Peter Lindbergh, showcasing model Michaela Bercu in a Christian Lacroix haute couture jacket paired unexpectedly with a sliver of Guess jeans. The headline boldly proclaimed, 'The real cost of looking good.' Bercu exuded confidence, wearing a big smile and sporting tousled hair. This juxtaposition of high fashion and casual denim was initially perceived as a deliberate fashion statement, signalling a move towards a high/low mix. However, Wintour later revealed that it was a serendipitous occurrence. Bercu couldn't fit into the skirt of the original Christian Lacroix suit, leading to the impromptu pairing with jeans. The photo, not initially intended for the cover, caught Wintour''s discerning eye. Recognising its compelling freshness and distinctiveness, she decided to feature it prominently, knowing it would spark conversation and make a memorable impact on her first works for Vogue.

'His British accent was definitely real.' We continued discussing him as we delved into exploring Venice. Marco, Sophia's photographer, joined us, capturing moments a few steps behind as we strolled through the floating city.

'You have to find out his name and his origins. You have to call him tonight.' I said, posing for a photo at the Salizada San Moisè.

'I know. Not just because of the Royal accent, but because he looked so darn good, didn't he?' I nodded in agreement. Sophia continued, 'And he was so pleasant and funny. But I was surprised that he didn't do the trick of dialling his number from my phone so he could have my number right away. I find that simpler, so he could call if he was interested and not just try being polite when I contact him.'

'I guess he thought the same about you. You didn't tell me; what did you talk about?' I asked, sensing the need to uncover the details of their conversation.

'It was a talk as impersonal as a newspaper,' she replied, her words leaving an air of mystery surrounding their discussion.

We both knew that Sophia had to find out more that night. The mysterious encounter sparked a curiosity that demanded satisfaction.

As we ventured deeper into the heart of Venice, the mesmerising charm of the city continued to cast its spell on us. Each step resonated with the echoes of centuries-old stories told through the magnificent architecture at every corner. The delicate fragrance of blooming flowers lingered in the air, wrapping us in a sensory embrace that heightened the romantic atmosphere. As we strolled along the winding canals, gondolas glided gracefully on the shimmering waters, their gondoliers expertly navigating the labyrinthine waterways. Playfully, the gondoliers would look at us with a smile, greet us in Italian, and express admiration with the familiar Italian gesture for beautiful women. We responded with laughter, finding the flirtation in Venice to be a natural and innocent expression of the spellbinding environment. The vibrant colours of the buildings lining the canals painted a lively backdrop, reminiscent of an artist's palette come to life.

Navigating the heart of the city's fashion district, we discovered boutiques that were seamlessly tucked between historic landmarks. In the shop windows, mannequins exuded sophistication, draped in the season's latest couture gowns. Each dress, a masterpiece, captured the essence of Venetian fashion with its flowing lines and intricate embellishments.
The displays beckoned with a diverse array of styles, ranging from classic sophistication to avant-garde chic. A parade of tailored suits embellished with subtle Venetian motifs shared the spotlight with ethereal dresses boasting delicate lace and

embroidery. Amidst the captivating creations, the spring collection stood out with its palette of pastel hues reminiscent of blooming flowers and intricate floral patterns that added a touch of seasonal whimsy.

As we continued our journey, the click-clack of our sandals on the cobblestone streets harmonised with the ambient sounds of bustling cafes and the lively cadence of conversations.

In the midst of this ethereal ambience, Sophia eagerly unravelled her vision for an upcoming fashion editorial. With the canals, bridges, and historic buildings of Venice as our backdrop, she envisioned a photoshoot that would blend Venetian history with contemporary haute couture. The idea of adding our touch to this visual masterpiece infused our exploration of Venice with an added thrill, transforming each moment into a story, our very own fashion tale amidst the alleys and waterways of Venice.

One of the famous names forever associated with Venice, embodying style, life, and a revolutionary impact on modern art, is Peggy Guggenheim. Surprisingly, she transformed the art world by curating rather than creating. Her legacy spans from fostering the works of Djuna Barnes and Jean Cocteau to supporting Mark Rothko and Jackson Pollock. Peggy dedicated her life to championing the avant-garde, a commitment that transcended her art collection and seeped into her personal wardrobe. Her extravagant jewellery and penchant for Schiaparelli's surrealist designs reflected her audacious approach to visuals. At a gallery opening, she boldly donned one earring designed by Tanguy and another by Alexander Calder, challenging the traditional boundaries between Surrealism and Abstraction.

On a different occasion, she arrived in a cellophane-wrapped gown crafted by her close friend Elsa Schiaparelli. She was extravagant both between the sheets and in her closet, unapologetically making bold statements wherever she went. Peggy's lifestyle mirrored her avant-garde spirit—she collected lovers, dogs, and art. While her style might differ significantly from mine and Sophia's, I couldn't help but appreciate the artistic flair she brought to fashion.

Of course, we couldn't pass up the chance to check out the famous Peggy Guggenheim Collection that day. The museum showcased Peggy Guggenheim's personal collection, housed within her former residence along the majestic Grand Canal. As the last private owner of a gondola in Venice, Peggy not only immersed herself in the city's vibrant art scene but also embraced its distinctive lifestyle. Her 'port' on the Grand Canal provided a stunning vista, granting her a front-row seat to the ebb and flow of Venetian life from her own private sanctuary. The courtyard, visible from the Grand Canal, featured a central bronze sculpture by Marino Marini titled The Angel of the City. My knowledge of this artwork stemmed from Peggy's memoir, *Out of This Century: The Informal Memoirs of Peggy Guggenheim.* The sculpture depicted a rider on a horse with arms outstretched, face turned skyward, and a rather notable feature—his colossal phallus. According to Peggy, on public holidays, when nuns passed her courtyard in a motorboat heading towards the prefecture opposite her house, she would humorously remove the phallus. The artist, in a stroke of ingenuity, had designed it as a separate and detachable feature.

While European and North American art from the twentieth century may not have been my primary interest, the visit to Peggy Guggenheim's museum proved to be a captivating experience. The collection showcased an array of renowned artists from that era, each contributing to a spectacular display of creativity. What truly fascinated me was not just the art, however, but the architectural marvel that housed these treasures.

The palazzo, as the Italians eloquently termed it, was a visual symphony of history and sophistication. The long, low, one-story structure, strategically positioned in the culturally and architecturally rich landscape of Venice, held an ageless charm. The facade, crafted from Istrian stone, told a story of transformation from white to ivory, both hues telling tales of their own. The clean lines of the building granted it a timeless charm. At the same time, the iron fence on the outside door and the many windows formed a perfect contrast, reminiscent of a refined Venetian checkerboard.

From a distance, the palazzo appeared as a piece of art in itself—a meticulous composition of precise lines and enduring style. The architecture reflected a deliberate choice as if the intention was to stand out from the conventional structures surrounding it. Interestingly, the building's height was a result of unforeseen circumstances. Initially planned as a five-story palace, only the first story was constructed. Locals amusingly referred to it as the palazzo non-finito—the unfinished palace. I did, however, find a sense of completion within it, almost as if the architect intended to showcase an unusual restraint that distinguished it from its counterparts.

Rumours lingered about the incomplete construction, with some suggesting that the foundations were not laid deep enough to support a five-storey palace. Equally plausible was the notion that the family's declining fortune or the absence of a new generation of male heirs brought the construction to a halt. The interruption was further compounded by Napoleon's invasion of Venice before the work could be resumed. The palazzo, frozen in time, stood as a captivating reflection of the intriguing intersection of history, architecture, and art.

The stage was set for a one-of-a-kind photo shoot, with me as the star dressed in a flowing black Schiaparelli gown featuring pearl-white silk rosette sleeves. The gown's colours and shape blended effortlessly with the timeless beauty of

Peggy's palazzo, forging a magical link between Peggy, Elsa Schiaparelli, Sophia, and myself—a mutual passion for fashion and the captivating city of Venice.

As Sophia diligently recorded her notes and the photographer captured the shots, I attempted to immerse myself in every breath of Venice. I quickly realised, however, that it wasn't easy to breathe in the narrow corset hugging my core. The thick, humid air wasn't doing me any favours, either.

Sophia was a perfectionist in her craft; she sought excellence in every photo—the ideal lighting, precise hand positioning, the perfect gesture and expression. The eyes had to smile, but not the lips. She had a flawless story in mind that needed to be visually translated. The stunning dress was a story in itself. Handmade in Italy with clear attention to detail, the photos had to capture its essence, reflecting the time and care put into its creation.

After the photo shoot, I treated myself to the flavours of the city. Have you ever tried the delightful chocolate Zaeti? Venice was no stranger to sweetness, especially with its early embrace of sugar, alongside the introduction of new fabrics and colours influenced by its maritime trade with the East.

That evening, an invitation led us to Gio's—a restaurant which famously encompassed an exquisite blend of modern and classic, seamlessly weaving together the essence of both the romantic Venice and the bustling New York. We were seated on the terrace—thanks to Sophia's ability to sweet talk the host—and the ambience was nothing short of magical. As the sun dipped below the horizon during the golden hour, the patio became the ideal spot to enjoy an aperitif.

Venice bathed in the soft glow of the setting sun, which seemed to solely possess the most beautiful golden hue in the world. Just like Venetian Blue, it was a shade that was uniquely Venetian. The Basilica San Marco, for instance, captured my fascination with its mosaics of bright half-suns—a sight unparalleled in my travels. What intrigued me even more was the way their colour transformed throughout the day. At midday, they gleamed in brilliant yellow; at sunset, bathed in the warm rays, they turned into burnished gold. This captivating transformation extended to much of the Romanesque and Gothic architecture that graced the city.

The Basilica San Marco, a haven of grandeur, shelters the Pala d'Oro—an altar crafted from solid gold and adorned with pearls, rubies, and amethysts. Measuring an impressive three metres wide and two metres high, the altar exudes a lavishness that may exceed my personal taste, but its sheer splendour is undeniably captivating. Notably, the Pala d'Oro stands as the world's sole remaining intact piece of large-scale Gothic goldsmith's art, adding a layer of historical intrigue to its ornate magnificence.

Gold has been a symbol of wealth and luxury for ages, and its charm still enchants the fashion world today. Italy, especially, has a strong link to gold, showcased by top Alta Moda designers like Dolce & Gabbana, Versace, and Roberto Cavalli. These fashion mavens effortlessly incorporate gold into their designs, whether it's through lavish fabrics or stunning accessories. Take Versace, for example; they love to showcase the iconic Medusa's head in gleaming gold. This stylised portrayal of Medusa, with her flowing snake hair and captivating gaze, exudes both beauty and a hint of danger. Just like the allure of gold, the image of Medusa has a magnetic and multifaceted quality that goes beyond the ordinary, prompting us to ponder the dynamics of strength, beauty, and luxury. Gold remains a powerful and valuable material, and reflecting on its enduring prominence in our society, one cannot help but marvel at its unchallenged position over the years.

The influence of gold extends beyond contemporary fashion, reaching back to the grandeur of the Roman Empire. Italy's illustrious past is intertwined with the enduring legacy of gold, a timeless element that continues to dazzle in the world of design. Venice, renowned for its fondness for gold, provides a striking example of the everlasting charm of this precious metal. During my first visit to Venice six or seven years ago, I stumbled upon a captivating local tradition dating back over a thousand years. On the day of Christ's Ascension, while the rest of Italy engages in festivities, the people of Venice turn their gaze towards the lagoon. A regatta, once led by the ceremonial golden barge known as the bucentaur during the era of the doges, sets sail for the monastery of San Nicolò al Lido. The mayor concludes the 'Marriage of the Sea' ceremony by ceremoniously casting a golden wedding ring into the shimmering waters, symbolically uniting Venice with the sea. For the doges, this event signified the celebration of Venice's maritime supremacy.

Unfortunately, the bucentaur met its demise at the hands of Napoleon, marking the French invasion of Venice. Despite this loss, the enduring tradition highlights the deep bond between Venice, its inhabitants, and the beloved gold.

Later that evening, the dress code called for black and gold, a palette chosen by Sophia, our designated stylist for the night. Gold isn't something you just casually throw on—it's reserved for those rare, special occasions when you're ready to shimmer and shine. My outfit was a simple yet chic ankle-length silk slip dress boasting a subtle slit that generously showcased my caged sandals wrapping around my calves. A hammered gold metal cuff adorned my upper arm, while my mid-sized creole earrings added a touch of Florentine elegance. The bracelet and earrings were the only pieces truly mine, not borrowed from Sophia's vast magazine wardrobe. By the end of the night, though, the sandals found a new home in my closet. My phone pouch, a classic black with a gold-toned chain and the iconic D&G logo, hung elegantly, carrying all the essentials— phone, lip liner, credit card, and a hefty hotel room key. I've always preferred the traditional key over the modern card, despite the occasional inconvenience when carrying a micro bag headed to a party. I hate it when I have made it to the twentieth-something floor in my hotel with a wet bikini and a bathrobe on with only one elevator in function, and the door opener blinks red, and I have to go back to the reception to exchange the card. It occurred to me later that evening that I could have lightened my clutch's load by leaving the key behind at the front desk.

Sophia opted for a chic yet almost classic look, donning a little black dress crafted from the iconic Alaia knit with a high-shine finish. The sleeveless silhouette gracefully followed the contours of her impeccable figure from the neckline to the waist, erupting into voluminous, three-dimensional stitches. Opting for Rockstud mules with transparent PVC wedge heels for her feet, Sophia made a thoughtful choice to navigate Venice's charming yet often challenging terrain. Completing the outfit, she wore a floor-length cape in the colour of an antique Roman coin.

The luminosity of gold radiates and complements the wearer's appearance, making it a universally flattering colour. Symbolically, gold dresses are associated with triumph and success. This symbolic significance is often observed among nominees aspiring to secure the top honours at high-profile award shows like the Oscars. In 1966, Julie Christie won the Best Actress award clad in a mod gold dress featuring a high-collar neckline. Gleaming as brightly as the Oscar itself, she complimented her look with gold statement earrings and a matching belt, creating a monochromatic look that harmonised with her shiny new accolade.

After dinner, we wandered through the narrow passageways of the Venetian streets. The city grew quieter as it embraced the serenity of the night. The gentle sounds of water lapping against the sides of the lagoon serenaded us. In the evening, Piazza San Marco seemed to expand, and although it was only 10:00 PM, Venice was settling into its nocturnal slumber.

Returning to our room overlooking the Grand Canal, I delicately removed the borrowed dress, placing it on the armchair beside the glimmering sandals, the gold-chained pouch, and the Roman-style arm cuff. As I carefully laid out the pieces, a thought crossed my mind: if Venice were a girl, this would undoubtedly be her signature style.

Sophia hailed a taxi. But this time, she did so via text.

CHAPTER FOUR

The Marie Antoinette mirror was my very first purchase upon moving into the apartment. In my previous flat, there wasn't enough wall space to house such a grand mirror, but I had always been drawn to its magnificence. To me, this mirror wasn't merely furniture; it was a statement. Reflecting the extravagant lifestyle of the final generation of the French Royal Family, it exuded grandeur with its size, added flair with its ornate details and glossy finish, and bore a name linked to a controversial reign that forever shaped French history.

Standing before my Marie Antoinette, I slipped on a pair of creole earrings, the mirror reflecting its richness within its ornate frame. It was astonishing how that mirror transformed my hallway, elevating not just the space but also my confidence. Amidst its luxurious setting, the mirror remained the apartment's focal point, a symbol of my fondness for the finer things.

As I adjusted my golden creole earring, Daniel, wearing nothing but a smile, wrapped his arms around me and pulled me close. The contrast between the mirror's grandeur and his warm embrace felt like merging history with intimacy—a rare occurrence in my home but unquestionably seductive.

While he was in Munich, Daniel stayed either at my place or at The Charles. We had been seeing each other almost every weekend for the last four months, and sometimes our time together extended to five consecutive days, each one more amazing than the last.

'Stay…' he whispered in my ear, his voice a soft caress.

'Oh, but I can't; I need to go and sell shoes so I can buy shoes. Do you recall that the first time we met, you approached me because of my shoes?' I recounted the memory with a playful tone, relishing the lightheartedness of our initial encounter.

Our paths first crossed at Heathrow in London, and while I initially believed it was a twist of fate, Daniel later revealed that he had taken matters into his own hands that day. Nevertheless, perhaps destiny still played a part in our story, as experts suggest that we may be destined to fall in love with certain people, even though it doesn't guarantee smooth sailing.

Somewhere between the security checkpoint and the boarding gate, our story unfolded. A striking man dressed in a white knit sweater, marine blue shorts, and Loro Piana beige cashmere loafers—clearly with a keen eye for fashion — complimented me on my sparkling flats. The flats, crafted in the famous H shape, showcased my freshly done ruby red pedicure and my tanned feet. I suspected he was referring to the overall aesthetic when he uttered, 'Stunning sandals.'

'Thank you,' I believe that was my response, and little did I know that this seemingly casual exchange would mark the beginning of a remarkable journey.

'I am flying to Munich, and I have an hour until boarding. Would you join me for lunch? I know a place with excellent burgers.' he asked me.

'I am flying to Munich too!' What a coincidence, I thought.

'What a coincidence!' He exclaimed as if he heard my inner conversation with his own ears. 'They don't have burgers like these in Munich. Will you trust me on this?'

I smiled, finding it hard to resist the combination of a handsome man and the promise of an excellent burger. Without warning, he grabbed my hand and led the way.

Though I certainly appreciate a good burger, and French fries are a personal favourite of mine, my recent inclinations have steered me away from enjoying meat. Opting for the vegetarian burger, I was pleasantly surprised to find that he made the same choice, creating an unexpected connection in our culinary preferences.

I learned that he lived in Hamburg and had business partners in Munich. I asked myself what kind of business partners he had to meet on weekends like this. But I didn't ask him. What he did with his business partners was none of my business. I had the best burger and fries ever at an airport restaurant. I remember the place had a modern yet cosy atmosphere, with dimmed lights and a playlist that made the fast-food eatery even feel quite romantic. The conversation flowed easily between us, and it almost felt like a first date. As we talked, I couldn't help but notice the way his eyes lit up when he discussed his travels and the excitement in his voice when he spoke about sailing. It was clear that he had a passion for life, and it was infectious.

After spending a few weekends together, he confessed that he had stolen a glimpse of my ticket on my phone screen in the security line. It was at that moment he came up with the idea to tell me that he was travelling to Munich, too. Initially, he wasn't. But then he decided he wanted to spend more time with me, so he booked a flight to Munich. Ingeniously, he even approached the gentleman sitting next to me, requesting a seat switch so we could sit together. It turned out he had booked the flight to Munich solely to be with me, revealing a sweet and unexpected gesture that touched my heart.

The day I met him at the airport and we flew together to Munich, we parted ways at the train station, he headed to The Charles, I to my apartment. But our separation was brief. Two hours later, we were reunited for an intimate dinner. Over dinner, I noticed with amusement how heartily he devoured his Ribeye, a stark contrast to the vegetarian burger he'd ordered at the airport.

'I was so engrossed in our conversation, I didn't even notice your order. You told the server, and I simply asked for the same. When the food arrived, I was surprised but secretly relieved. Maybe you're a hardcore vegetarian, and ordering meat would have been a red flag. I'm not a meat enthusiast myself; I prefer fries too. But why didn't you say something when I suggested burgers?"

'You said excellent burgers. And when the burgers are good, the French fries are usually pretty good, too,' I responded. 'That's pretty much all I care about anyway.'

'Does it bother you if someone else eats meat?' he asked.

'I believe everyone should make their own choices. It just feels so unfair that we get to decide their lives for them. They are living creatures too, just like us.'

After dinner and cocktails at The Charles, I returned home, eager for the next day. That weekend, the dimly lit bar and worn leather seats of The Charles transformed into our own Casablanca, a sanctuary for late-night confessions. Dreams, fears, aspirations—everything spilled out. Talking to him felt effortless. He seemed genuinely captivated by everything I shared, even the most mundane details.

The outside world faded as we delved deep into conversation. Even a theatre outing at the Bayerischer Hof became a talking marathon. Who needs a full play when you have such captivating company? This wasn't just about stolen glances and picturesque walks; it was about rapid, complete intimacy.

He returned to Hamburg on Monday. Alone at the theatre that evening, I watched the play to its end. Although the show was not particularly hilarious, I found myself laughing a lot, solely because I admitted to myself that I was falling in love.

The feeling was as unexpected as it was delightful. Love, with its quirky timing, had quietly tiptoed into my life, catching me off guard yet again. The mundane scenes of everyday life were now tinted with a rosy hue, and the ordinary had transformed into the extraordinary. As I sat in the dimly lit theatre, I reflected on the intimate moments shared over the weekend—the laughter, the conversations, and the subtle sparks that hinted at something more profound.

The play served as a backdrop to my introspection, and I couldn't help but appreciate the serendipity that had brought us together. Love's arrival was like a subtle crescendo, building gradually until it resonated through every heartbeat. It was a rhythm I hadn't anticipated but one I was eager to explore further. As the final curtain dropped and the theatre erupted in applause, I couldn't shake the thought: Did he feel the same electric connection as I did? And, of course, what will the girls think of him?

...

'So, he made up a story about his flight? To hit on you? Elena, he is capable of lying. Watch out,' as I retold the story, my pragmatic friend Sophia whisked me away from the seventh heaven and brought me back to Earth.

'Don't be so dramatic. I find his storytelling a bit silly, but there's a certain romantic charm to it,' I responded, acknowledging the whimsy in his narrative.

'It is charming. But it's still a lie,' she continued, highlighting the tension between the appeal of a romantic tale and the truth that underlies it.

After her last experience, she became even more sceptical of men. I didn't think it was possible, but there she was —my highly predictable friend—with her heart completely closed off to the idea that true love could enter her life again. Or her best friend's life.

Sophia's scepticism was a shield she wore, a protective layer against the potential heartaches that love might bring. I understood her caution, but my heart was still basking in the glow of newfound emotions. Love, with its unpredictability, had caught me by surprise, and I was willing to take the risk.

'I'll be careful, Sophia. But sometimes, you have to let go of the fear to welcome something beautiful,' I said, hoping my words would find a way to soften the walls around her heart.

She sighed. 'I just don't want to see you hurt, especially not by a man who might weave tales for his own amusement.'

As we delved into a deeper conversation about love, trust, and the complexities of human connections, I couldn't help but ponder the delicate dance between caution and vulnerability that defined our approach to matters of the heart.

Despite Sophia's warnings lingering in the back of my mind, I found solace in the genuine moments we shared. Daniel's attentiveness made me feel desired, and with him, I experienced desire to the fullest. Love, like the intricate designs of Venetian lace, required patience and craftsmanship. I was ready to unravel its mysteries, one delicate thread at a time, even if it meant confronting the uncertainties that lay ahead. The echoes of Sophia's caution wavered, but in the heart's quiet chambers, the symphony of love played on, and I didn't mind swaying to its rhythm.

...

Just recently, I had explored further into the intriguing story of 14-year-old Marie Antoinette. En route to France for her marriage to King Louis XVI, the border between Austria and France marked a symbolic threshold. Here, she changed from her Austrian attire into French garments—a carefully orchestrated gesture designed to make a striking first impression in her new home.

My sentiments toward Marie Antoinette were complex. I admired the uniqueness of both my ornate mirror and Marie herself. Her strength of will, audacity, and unwavering commitment to high fashion, even when impractical, commanded respect. However, she stood as a stark contrast to sustainable fashion, earning her title as the Queen of Excess during France's financial crises. Legend has it that she acquired approximately 300 gowns each year.

Upon arriving in France, Marie embraced the emerging Rococo style characterised by pale pastel-toned silks, voluminous layered skirts, and ornate decorative elements such as jewels, ribbons, and ruffles. The skirts, often supported by side hoops, created a dramatic silhouette around the hips. They were notoriously impractical, expanding to ridiculous proportions, sometimes up to five metres in diameter. Conversely, the waists were cinched tightly into restricting corsets, resulting in a relatively flat front and back.

Emilia Schuele, the talented actress who played the role of Marie Antoinette in the eponymous drama, shared insights into the challenges of portraying the iconic queen. Reflecting on the corsets worn for authenticity, she candidly remarked, 'It was great preparation for the character because you really suffer.' Her acknowledgement sheds light on the dedication and sacrifice Marie Antoinette underwent to achieve her desired look.

Marie Antoinette's profound preoccupation with clothing went beyond mere fashion. It served as a powerful means of self-expression. One iconic portrait featuring her in the scandalous chemise-style gown became a focal point of public outrage in pre-revolutionary France. In the eyes of 18th-century society, this choice was interpreted as a direct insult. Marie's unwitting popularisation of fabrics from colonised India, instead of endorsing French silk, was perceived as a highly unpatriotic act. This seemingly innocuous preference had the potential to not only harm the French silk market but also, in the larger context, contribute to the unravelling of the monarchy itself during the tumultuous era of the French Revolution.

CHAPTER FIVE

'Leave a little sparkle wherever you go.'

This was Veronica encapsulated in a phrase. As expected, Xavier coined the nickname Tinker Bell, and soon, it became a playful moniker embraced by everyone in the boutique. It was our little inside joke, a term of endearment shared among us. Veronica, the source of inspiration for the nickname, was unaware of our playful banter, but I doubted it would bother her even if she knew. After all, she was more than just a customer to us; she served as a vibrant presence that added a touch of magic to the shop.

However, we were cautious about using nicknames with customers, adhering to a level of professionalism. In our interactions, names were seldom used. It made me ponder, dear reader, have you ever wondered what your nickname might be at your favourite boutique? The relationships we build with sales associates are two-way streets founded on mutual respect. Treat them with the same courtesy they extend your way, and you'll likely find yourself with a nickname that resonates.

Building genuine rapport with the staff at your favourite boutique isn't simply about good manners but rather about fostering a connection that is more than just transactional. When you reciprocate their warmth and respect, you create an environment where mutual appreciation flourishes. So, the next time you strut into your fashion haven, remember that the way you treat the staff can determine whether you leave with a nickname that brings a smile to your face or one that leaves you scratching your head.

Veronica was our Tinker Bell. She possessed a slender figure, standing a bit shorter than average, yet her impeccable posture and graceful gait bestowed an aura of timeless elegance upon her. One thing that always caught my attention was her shoulder-length icy-blond hair, consistently looking as if it had just been styled. I couldn't help but wonder about the secrets of her hair care routine. But it was her sapphire blue eyes that were truly something to behold, the most striking feature of her perfectly symmetrical face. Even the freckles gracing her fair complexion seemed strategically placed. When she flashed her signature smile, her eyes lit up with contagious joy, outshining even her lips, casting a spell that made it nearly impossible to look away. While Veronica might not have fit the conventional standards of beauty, her unique charm was undeniable.

Although she was a new customer, it didn't take long for Veronica to transition into a regular. Her purchases reflected impeccable taste in shoes, purchasing two pairs of 100 mm slingbacks, one pair of 100 mm stilettos, one pair of mules, and one pair of over-the-knee boots. In essence, Veronica's choices spoke volumes about her discerning eye for fashion, making her a welcomed presence in the boutique.

Veronica was soft-spoken and had an inherently polite nature. Each time she visited the boutique, she would greet me with a genuine inquiry about my day and plans for the weekend. Despite her warmth, she never sought my opinion on the shoes she tried on; instead, she possessed an unwavering confidence in her own taste. I appreciated that about her.

Her shopping approach was both calculated and efficient. Veronica knew precisely what she wanted and never hesitated to express it in the most courteous way possible, of course. With a keen awareness of which shoe models complemented her style, she would decisively affirm, 'Yes, these sandals are definitely me,' or dismiss a pair with a polite, 'No, I would love to bring them home, but I know I wouldn't wear them.' How brilliant is that! I couldn't help but admire her level-headedness, a quality I often wished to emulate during my own shopping excursions. She didn't experiment with colours either, always sticking to black.

But wait, the mules she got were white! It marked a delightful departure from her usual colour, revealing a subtle willingness to embrace versatility. Her wardrobe, too, predominantly revolved around the monochromatic duo of black and white. Yet, whether in black, white, or a fusion of both, she radiated in those hues like no one else I knew. The timeless combination, far from seeming ordinary, invariably managed to set her apart.

Actually, black is such a happy colour. It makes us appear slimmer, and that makes us happy. Beyond the mere aesthetic, black establishes itself as a chameleon in the world of fabrics, seamlessly adapting to a diverse array of textures and materials. Whether donning the elegance of a sleek evening gown, the precision of a tailored suit, or the simplicity of casual everyday wear, its universal charm remains undeniable. It looks serious. It looks chic. It looks modest. It looks rebellious. It looks good with all skin tones and with every hair colour. It just looks good.

The everlasting appeal of the colour black in the fashion industry shows just how timeless and versatile the shade is in nature. Dispelling the notion that vibrant and experimental designs dominate the high-fashion landscape, black remains a consistent presence on the catwalks, a steadfast staple that defies the capricious nature of trends. Like a felt-tip marker in the same shade, black is permanent.

Esteemed designers such as Azzedine Alaia, Comme des Garçons, and Ann Demeulemeester continue to weave stories of black into their collections. Yohji Yamamoto, known for his avant-garde approach to design, harnesses the power of black to accentuate intricate proportions and cuts and uses it as a canvas that directs attention to the form and texture of the garments rather than distracting with multiple-hued patterns.

Black has been a formidable statement in the hands of iconic creators like Cristóbal Balenciaga and Yves Saint Laurent, as well. Balenciaga employs black for its elegant, architectural silhouettes, while Saint Laurent disrupts norms with the groundbreaking le smoking women's tuxedo. Both designers harness the unique qualities of black to create a striking sense of individuality—despite using a colour that is so common.

The adaptability and charm of black have etched its place as a perennial favourite on the couture panorama. As Christian Dior emphasised in his 1954 book 'The Little Dictionary of Fashion,' black transcends the constraints of time, age, and occasion. It stands as an uncompromising choice that effortlessly graces any hour of the day or night.

Beyond its visual appeal, black's rich history and cultural significance contribute to its multifaceted symbolism in fashion and beyond. An all-black ensemble—often regarded as a sophisticated and classic statement—carries diverse meanings throughout history. Historically, the colour black and its dark counterparts are associated with notions of evil, death, eroticism, piety, and puritanism. But black's significance evolves with the passage of time— and today, it symbolises much more than the 'absence of colour'. In times past, individuals experiencing grief and loss would don black as a symbolic expression of grief, particularly during the Victorian era when mourning attire became a nuanced system of visual communication. As such, this type of messaging demanded specific fabrics and clothing styles which indicated different stages of mourning, ultimately creating a complex language of its own.

The cultural history of black clothing began as a symbol of wealth and status among Europe's elite, and is now a widely embraced fashion choice accessible to all. In the past, creating black dyes was an intricate and costly process, contributing to its exclusivity and association with affluence. It became a quintessential tell for sophistication, starting with Spanish nobility in the south and Dutch merchants in the north.

The Victorian era witnessed a transformation in the availability of black clothing with the development of cheaper dyes, which broadened access to black garments. This democratisation made black more prevalent and popular among diverse social classes.

The early 20th century marked a significant shift in the perception of black as a fashion choice. Socialites embraced the trend of little black dresses, using this chic and versatile wardrobe staple to convey a sense of youthfulness and edginess. This shift further popularised the colour black as a reliable style essential.

Traditionally worn by religious orders, black attire reflects a sense of seriousness and diligence. On the flip side, it can also evoke an ominous or defiant connotation, as seen with the cloaks of witches or the leather jackets associated with biker gangs. And beyond its historical associations, black has become a powerful symbol of protest in contemporary contexts. Instances like the 2018 Golden Globes awards ceremony demonstrate its capacity to convey solidarity and resistance. Attendees, particularly actresses and actors, arrived in all-black looks as a visual expression of support for the Time's Up and #MeToo movements, a powerful statement against habitual sexual harassment in Hollywood and beyond. In this way, black transcends its purely aesthetic appeal and becomes a tool for social and political expression.

From a purely scientific standpoint, black isn't classified as a colour; rather, it represents the absence of all visible wavelengths, standing in a category of its own. Even so, this characteristic doesn't diminish its cultural relevance and popularity in fashion. A recent analysis looking into the sale of approximately 200,000 dresses online in the U.S. uncovered a striking trend: over one-third of dresses sold were some shade of black, cementing its position as the most sought-after colour available. In contrast, the second-most popular colour, white, accounted for only about 10% of the dresses sold.

Coco Chanel's legendary signature is the perfect blend of black and white - an iconic, effortless pairing that has transcended eras. This revered colour combination has become inextricably intertwined with the brand's sophisticated, timeless image, rendering it as modern today as it was visionary at its inception. Coco Chanel's influence on the world of fashion is immeasurable, and her declaration about these two shades resonates to this day. 'Women think of all colours except the absence of colour. I have said that black has it all. White too. Their beauty is absolute. It is the perfect harmony,' she proclaimed. Amen, indeed.

Nora Ephron's humorous take on black in her book I Feel Bad About My Neck perfectly captures the universal charm of this colour: 'Black looks great on older women with dark hair– so great, in fact, that even younger women with dark hair wear black. Even women in L.A. wear black... Everything matches black. Especially black.'

This chapter was meant to be about Veronica, but it nearly turned into an ode to the colour black. Just as it is for fashion designers, black was a significant inspiration for me, as well. Veronica. I know my clients well, and I knew that Veronica's preference for black and white showcased her refined taste. Or, so I thought. The truth is, do we ever truly know the people we think we know?

The simplicity of the classic hues she wore everyday became an unexpected canvas for her charismatic personality to shine through like the vibrant colours of the rainbow on an overcast day.

'Any plans for the weekend?' she asked casually, sinking into the jet-black velvet armchair.

'Not really. My boyfriend is coming to Munich, so I'm just looking forward to spending time with him,' I replied, handing her a pair of slingbacks in iridescent silk chiffon. Black, of course.

'You have a new boyfriend?' she inquired, swiftly adding: 'You don't have this style in other colours at the moment, do you?'

The questions caught me off guard. Which other colour than black could she possibly want, and when did I talk to her about my last relationship? Tinker Bell seemed to notice my hesitation and clarified, 'I saw them online in white.'

'Oh, white. No, but I can order it to the store if you want.'

Okay, white was acceptable for Tinker Bell. But I was still jarred by her question about my 'new boyfriend'. She didn't press further, and I didn't vocalise my confusion about her curiosity, either.

'Yes, please. I'll take them in both shades, actually. They are absolutely my style.' Her attention was focused intently on the shoes as if the world beyond them had momentarily slipped away.

She was right; her style was simple yet feminine. She radiated an understated grace that effortlessly complemented her personality. Unlike some of my other clients, Veronica never spoke about herself, and I respected that by never probing into personal details. It made me wonder what stories lay behind her composed exterior, what passions and dreams she kept hidden beneath that serene surface. Frankly, the only significant thing I knew about her was her shoe size.

However, very soon, without any direct inquiries, I stumbled upon something I least expected.

CHAPTER SIX

The next day, the shipment I was expecting with Tinker Bell's white slingbacks arrived at the store. Talk about customer service; that was fast. I was just texting Veronica about the good news when Javier's older sister, Isabella, stopped by for a visit. I couldn't help but notice their reserved behaviour, which hinted at a reunion long overdue. According to Javier, they hadn't seen each other for more than a year, and his eagerness to introduce Isabella to his newly embraced Munich family prompted him to bring her to the store for a formal introduction. It was heartwarming to see how proud Javier was to show her around. Their physical similarities were obvious. Every characteristic, from the shared dark brown—almost black—curls, with Javier's cascading slightly shorter than Isabella's, to the matching deep, enigmatic eyes and the high nose with a charming ridge, was the same. And yet, they each were perfectly beautiful and attractive in their own unique ways.

As conversations deepened and the minutes unfolded in the familiar ambience of the store, it became apparent that the siblings were like distinct pairs of shoes from separate and curated collections, each representing a different fashion epoch. Their dynamic was truly as a captivating juxtaposition—Isabella embodied Prêt-à-Porter practicality, while her brother, Javier, was unmistakably haute couture. She was the epitome of Minimalism, and he, an embodiment of the opulent Art Deco era.

What I found most interesting was that Isabella radiated an air of strict reserve that rendered her presence intriguing, if slightly challenging—unlike her brother. Conversations with her felt like putting on an interpretive performance, leaving you uncertain whether she failed to grasp your joke or just didn't find it funny. Though we had just scratched the surface of getting to know one another, her genuine concern for Javier was revealed. It was evident that the sheer geographical distance between them weighed heavily on her heart, and she missed being so close to family. Plus, Isabella's dedication to her role as a caring sister was obvious. Her protective instincts were subtly conveyed in her expressions and the way she cautiously examined his chosen family here in Munich. In those brief moments, she not only showcased her role as a good sister but excelled in articulating it, at least from my perspective.

'I've done everything you asked for,' I overheard her declare with a determined tone.

'But how could you have known what I truly wanted? You never asked, never lent an ear. That, above all, was what I craved—a confidante, someone willing to genuinely listen,' came the poignant response from her brother.

'I went to great lengths to secure Father's acceptance of you, just as you are,' she replied.

'But did you ever accept me for who I am? We were the ones that grew up together, shared our secrets, fears, and passions. Father lives in a bygone era; I looked to you for understanding, knowing I wouldn't find it in him,' Javier responded; he was clearly frustrated.

I wanted to keep from interrupting them, but their voices grew louder. There were clients in the boutique with important issues to solve, too, such as choosing the perfect shoes or determining the right size. The staff—Javier's colleagues—urgently needed to redirect their attention to these matters. He may not have been on the clock, but we were.

In the grand story of life, siblings play a crucial role. No matter where life takes us, the bond with our siblings remains unyielding. Memories of growing up together continue to bring joy and comfort, much like a familiar melody. They are sometimes the only people we have for our whole life. Friends come later, and parents leave too early. If we are fortunate, our siblings will always have our back, sharing in life's highs and lows from start to finish. It's the laughter at family gatherings, the playful reminiscing of childhood adventures, and the unwavering support through thick and thin. It's important to celebrate these enduring bonds and cherish the irreplaceable essence they bring to our lives.

I empathised deeply with Javier. His disappointment and sense of exclusion from his family were palpable, but I couldn't help but wonder if his perception might be skewed. Was he perhaps expecting acceptance without reciprocating it? He said that his family never accepted him as he was. But did he take his family as they were? His family, proud and steeped in tradition, had an antiquated mindset, and Javier's frustration seemed to stem from the clash of his expectations with their entrenched values. Sometimes, the path to harmony involves accepting others as they are and leading by example so that they might follow suit.

After Isabella's parting wave faded into the distance, Javier turned to me, his expression etched with hurt and disbelief. 'She travelled all this way, yet not a single apology passed her lips,' he said, his voice strained by the weight of his emotions. 'She really hurt me. Doesn't she know that?' His eyes met mine, silently pleading for an answer, an explanation, a remedy for the ache that I could not provide.

I sighed, thinking, why didn't you tell her that? Instead, I said 'Life becomes more manageable when you learn to accept an apology you never received. Try considering her journey here as an unspoken apology in itself,' I went on. 'Sometimes, understanding and forgiveness pave the way for healing. Sometimes it surpasses the need for explicit words of remorse.'

I said nothing new. It's a truth we all recognise but often find challenging to live by.

Javier was settling well into his new life in Munich. He was content with his job, and he was excelling at it. I also knew he had been redecorating his apartment to suit his style instead of the previous owner's. Most exciting of all, there was the presence of someone he had met and who was becoming very special to him. Unfortunately, that special someone already had a special one in his life. Her name was Lisa.

'I hate that he has a dog. I am not fur-friendly. Not as a material for any of my clothing, and definitely not when it's on a real creature,' Javier responded without a second thought.

'Have you seen your legs?' I joked. Javier was known for his sophisticated demeanour but was notably unyielding in his stance against body waxing.

'Very funny. I just don't like waking up alone because the guy has to walk his dog at six in the morning. Neither do I relish being limited to only pet-friendly hotels or opting for a quiet night in rather than enjoying a lavish dinner at a fancy restaurant because it's more convenient for his dog. He dedicates so much time to his canine companion that I worry he's forgotten how to communicate with men.'

While Javier's grievances were valid, I wondered if he might be overreacting again. He was caught between his preferences and the nuances of a relationship that embraced not just two but three different parties.

'But if he has a dog, that also means that he can take responsibility and commit to someone,' I tried to inject a positive perspective, given the circumstances.

'Sure, he can commit to someone who can't talk back. The last time we had a fight—or, actually, I was having a fight—he just called his dog, she came running to him, and they both left. I'm confident if that dog could understand my words, she would never speak to me again,' Javier vented.

'Poor thing. Dogs will always side with their best friend no matter what,' I giggled.

'And the best friend is the one giving it treats, I assume?' Javier seemed annoyed, but I sensed there was more beneath the surface.

'A dog knows who its best friend is. And yes, treats are important in every relationship,' I started, identifying a venue to offer up some relationship advice. 'You know what? I think you should spoil him tonight. Cook something for him. Suggest staying at home since you know he prefers that. Be kind to his dog because she was there first. Think of it this way: for you, it will be easy to find a new partner. But not for that dog. There are a lot of single men who are looking for a gorgeous, smart man with a Spanish accent like you. But there aren't many that are willing to adopt a homeless dog. That dog has it more difficult than you,' I pointed out, nudging Javier toward a more holistic outlook.

'I know you're right. I'll get some treats for the dog, too,' Javier finally showed a genuine smile, signalling a willingness to bridge the gap and find harmony within the complexities of his budding relationship.

'Perfect. Just don't leave any precious shoes lying on the floor,' I winked at my friend before descending the steel staircase to the storage room. My mission? To uncover the elusive 100 mm red pumps with a mirrored finish in size 37. After all the socialisation, I had to get back to work. I looked at the pending requests for the day, and a familiar client name popped up. He was constantly visiting our store to spoil his family with what I assumed to be their favourite gift to receive: a new pair of shoes. As per the customer's order note, these shoes were intended to be a surprise for a special graduation day. The accompanying card contained a heartfelt message:

May your accomplishments continue to soar to even greater heights in the future and beyond. To my stylish daughter.

Love, Papa.

Family is a gift that lasts forever. They are our guiding light through life's triumphs and tribulations, the first people we turn to in joy, sorrow, and all the moments in between. Our family members are confidants, cheerleaders, and the bedrock upon which we build our lives. The true significance of family lies not just in shared bloodlines but in the profound connections we cultivate, the cherished memories we enshrine, and the enduring love that binds our souls together. It is this love that shapes our identities, moulding us into the people we are and aspire to become. And as we stand on the threshold of a new chapter, such as our graduation day, we are reminded that family is the foundation upon which we build our future. Imagine, years after that milestone, whenever that girl opens her closet and reaches for those crimson red heels—a graduation gift from her father—she will be transported back to that momentous day. With each step in those shoes, she'll be reminded of how amazing it is to have a family that stands by her side, unconditionally supporting her dreams and aspirations. How amazing it is to have those shoes.

And that's what made my job so special—bringing joy and magic to those moments, making them unforgettable. Whether it's a milestone celebration or a quiet, everyday moment, I was honoured to be a part of creating special memories that will last a lifetime.

CHAPTER SEVEN

To me, Sophia was the sister I never had. A quiet confidante who possessed the ancient art of listening and offering a response only when she sensed my need for one. There were moments when I simply craved an open ear, and without prompting, she'd let me pour my thoughts into the conversation while she maintained a thoughtful silence. Yet, she had an intuitive knack for figuring out when I needed her opinion. In those instances, she would gauge whether I wanted the hard truth or a sounding board for my own views on a situation.

I wasn't prepared to confront the possibility that he might have a girlfriend in Hamburg. Perhaps they were even sharing a life together, given the conspicuous absence of invitations for me to spend a weekend with him. Our FaceTime sessions were exclusively confined to office hours, and his sudden early bedtimes, coupled with abrupt silences, fueled my suspicions. Based on the past several months of us growing closer, I found myself developing genuine feelings for him. Intensely so.

After I laid out these details, Sophia, with a discerning look, asked me if I was ready for the unvarnished truth. With a hesitant nod, I signalled my consent, and she advised me to afford him a bit more time.

'More red flags will surface if your suspicions end up holding weight. But I genuinely don't believe they will. He strikes me as a reasonable guy. Having someone like you and jeopardising that connection doesn't seem reasonable,' she said with a measured tone, acknowledging my reluctance to let things be. She understood that I wasn't ready to suppress my feelings for him and that, despite my nod for the truth, the possible truth might be a bitter pill to swallow.

After parting ways with Maurice, Sophia had become somewhat disheartened with romance. She moved with a hesitant gait as if she were tiptoeing around the shards of her own broken heart. Still, I could tell the Englishman she encountered in Venice brought a renewed sense of hope and a sparkle to her eyes. 'He's…different,' she said as she came back from their date and rolled into our shared bed that night in Venice. 'Giorgo is warm, funny, and genuinely interested in who I am as a person.' Sophia let out a dreamy sigh, hugging a pillow to her chest. At that moment, I knew the date had gone surprisingly well—so well that she was opening herself up to love's possibilities again.

Their first date had unfolded in a small bistro on the corner of Saint Stephen's Place. At the restaurant, she discovered that his roots traced back to Sardinia, but that he was born and raised in London's posh Mayfair district. An Italian soul with a dapper English upbringing. A fascinating contradiction.

This explained his Italian appearance, coupled with a distinctly British accent. Engaged in the trade of exclusive furniture from his homeland, he sailed between Burano and Venice that day, introducing us to his boat (which he clarified was not a taxi boat), co-owned with a friend in the sustainable fabric business for the production of shoes.

Thus far, I found both him and his friend agreeable, and more importantly, so did Sophia. He embodied the gentlemanly qualities of an Englishman—polite and attentive—but he also embraced the adventurous and free-spirited nature characteristic of an Italian. That night, Sophia told me, as he bid Sophia farewell in front of our hotel, he left a lasting impression by not only kissing her hand but also squeezing it affectionately.

His parting words carried a subtle but profound message as he urged her, 'Live a little. Working is great, but it should not be the only thing that matters in your life.'

As Sophia recounted the British Italian's insightful observation, her surprise mirrored my own astonishment that neither of us had recognised this tendency earlier. Given our shared understanding that work had become the paramount focus in her life, it dawned on me that Alessia and I, as her closest friends, had been somewhat complicit in allowing this myopic fixation to persist unchecked. We should have cautioned her sooner that her conversations too often revolved solely around work, to the point where it could come across as more concerning than impressive to others. We should have made more concerted efforts to remind her of the vibrant array of other subjects she used to be passionate about before work began to dominate her life.

Still, he asked if he could see her the next day. Sophia expressed her willingness but mentioned our tight schedule during this work trip. Rather than insisting, he accepted her response gracefully. Sophia pondered whether his lack of insistence stemmed from excessive politeness or just disinterest.

The following morning at breakfast, a waiter delivered two glasses of champagne to our table, distinct from the buffet offerings. Attached to one glass was a handwritten note.

```
After you finish breakfast, meet me outside.
Work can wait. Venice and I cannot.
```

It was undeniably not meant for me. Sophia turned to me, 'What should I do?'

I responded by posing the question back to her, 'What do you want to do?'

Without hesitation, she downed her drink, rose from her seat, and swiftly declared, 'See you later! And don't forget we have tickets for the show. We have to be ready at six!'

I didn't see her until the next day for breakfast.

...

I didn't see Daniel until our weekend in Vienna. He happened to be in the city for work. I happened to be there for him. Arriving in Vienna on Thursday night, the train ride gave me time to plan a romantically orchestrated rendezvous. But it wasn't wholly romantic, considering my regional manager caught wind of my trip and scheduled a Friday meet-up with our Vienna Store team for a creative exchange. I didn't particularly mind it, though, considering the remainder of the days were dedicated to immersing myself in the city's charms and basking in the comforting embrace of Daniel's love.

The train pulled into the main station, and there was Daniel, reliable as a Swiss watch. Our walk to the hotel was a sensory overload—the Viennese streets thrumming with the soundtrack of Mozart and Strauss, the air thick with the intoxicating aroma of freshly baked Sacher torte. Everything seemed perfectly choreographed for a romantic weekend in one of Europe's most charming capitals.

The grand hotel entrance extended before us like a portal to another era. Stepping inside, I was transported to a gilded dream, a La Bohème set come to life. Marble floors gleamed like polished gemstones beneath the soft glow of crystal chandeliers, and plush armchairs whispered stories of bygone soirees. In contrast, my travel outfit suddenly felt decidedly uninspired as I stood there clinging to Daniel's arm like it was a life raft amidst the baroque splendour. I couldn't help but wonder... was this baroque fantasy Daniel's idea of romance? An over-the-top gesture to woo me with Old World charm? Or was the city itself seducing us with its irresistible mix of glamour and endearing class? Either way, pressed against the comforting solidness of his shoulder, I felt that delicious fluttering a girl only gets when she's truly, madly, falling.

'Ready for dinner?' Daniel showed me the way to the elevator. It seemed that he knew the place well.

'Not quite yet, but please give me the room keys and ten minutes, and I will be.'

'Absolutely. But be quick—we wouldn't want to miss our reservation,' he said with a chuckle and a wink. I wasn't sure what the joke was, but I cracked a smile at the sight of him finding something so amusing.

The elevator doors opened to reveal an ornate bench on the far side and velvet upholstered walls. We turned a corner and my eyes were pointed downward as we walked, analysing the beauty in the carpet itself. I had stayed at some beautiful hotels throughout my life, but the interior details throughout this one were truly spectacular.

Finally, we arrived at our room. He swung open the door to the suite, revealing a tastefully adorned space with a cosy ambience. Eager to immerse myself in the atmosphere, I momentarily set aside my suitcase to rush towards the balcony. As I stepped outside, I was greeted by a breathtaking view that included a small bistro table adorned with an unexpected surprise. Fresh oysters sat on a bed of ice, their briny aroma intermingling with the enticing scent of crispy french fries. The tableau was framed by an expansive panorama that generously showcased St. Charles Church's majestic baroque outfit.

'How does a night in sound to you?' he cooed, clearly proud that he pulled this off.

'It sounds perfect. I'm so glad we made our reservation after all,' I giggled. The french fries were still warm.

With the city's iconic landmark as our backdrop, he gracefully poured two glasses of Austrian rosé. The clink of our glasses resonated in the air. Whether the toast was dedicated to us or the promising weekend ahead remained a delightful ambiguity. I suppose it was the latter, as toasting 'to us' felt either too premature, or belated, in hindsight.

The evening unfolded with a sumptuous main course of fettuccine with lobster, setting the stage for a night filled with passion.

As dawn broke, we awoke to a shifted atmosphere, embracing the serenity of the morning. We lingered over an unhurried breakfast, the table cleared of last night's indulgent remnants and reset with fragrant jasmine tea, refreshing carrot juice, and a wholesome spread of granola in oat milk and berries. Energised and content, our bodies and souls feeling equally replenished, we left the hotel together, ready to head in different directions—both for work, carrying with us the lingering warmth of a shared and tranquil morning.

The Vienna store was a vision of a modern fairytale and surpassed even the captivating photos I had seen a few days prior. The location underwent a meticulous renovation process, which was completed piece by piece without ever fully closing its doors. Once unveiled, it was clear that each section had received careful attention, resulting in an interior that radiated contemporary opulence. As I explored the boutique before the store opened for the day, I smiled and greeted the interior designer who was there, adding her final touches, one of which included repositioning a vast mirror adorning the central wall. To my surprise, she seemed taken aback when I mentioned having the same mirror at home. Perhaps she hadn't anticipated that someone working at the store could afford such furniture.

The truth was, many of my indulgent purchases did surpass the limits of my monthly salary. However, my financial portfolio was a different story. Long before investing in luxurious furniture and exquisite shoes, I had wisely ventured into stocks, funds, and real estate. It wouldn't have been possible the other way around.

I discovered that the creative mind behind the boutique's interior belonged to a woman named Katharina, hailing all the way from the picturesque landscapes of Iceland. And even though she came from a colder region, the interior of the store was hot. Sophistication with a feisty red-gold touch. Her design prowess spoke volumes; she created an inviting ambience that beckoned visitors into a world of style and magic.

'I work mostly with Italian furnishings,' I recall her saying. Italian furnishings and French mirrors, apparently.

But I do seek inspiration from the country I grew up in,' she continued. 'It's a land of contrasts, with blue-ice glacier lagoons, steaming geysers, fiery volcanoes belching lava, and the Northern Lights shimmering in the night sky. A place with 24 hours of daylight in midsummer and long, dark hours in winter. But even in that darkness, there's a fantastic glow—just like this mirror. Covered in silver leaf and finished with a high-gloss varnish, it makes the black mahogany sparkle, especially under this light.' She concluded her speech, clearly proud to share her inspiration with someone who appreciated it.

'I see what you mean,' I said, genuinely interested. 'Though I have to admit, I'm surprised to see a mirror like this in a shoe store. I could picture it more in a beauty salon or a makeup store, where the focus is on the upper body.' I couldn't help but glance around the boutique, taking in the unexpected fusion of high-end shoes and the striking mirror.

'It's a mirror that makes you feel good. It represents an attitude of self-confidence—to be whoever you want to be and live your life however you want to. It's inspired by the controversy surrounding Marie Antoinette and her extravagant lifestyle,' she paused, stroking her chin in thought. 'It also has a connection with a fairytale. "Mirror, mirror on the wall, who's the fairest of them all?"' Katharina concluded her thought by looking in the mirror. To me, it seemed like she was waiting as if the mirror would really reply.

I never thought I would encounter Marie Antoinette in the city of Sisi, yet there she stood amidst the most exquisite pairs of shoes I had ever laid eyes on—the Autumn/Winter Collection. Timeless styles with equestrian-inspired silhouettes lined the shelves. From knee-high boots with pointed toes perched on daring stiletto heels to chic lace-up ankle boots boasting lug rubber soles for cold-weather adventures. Eye-catching over-the-knee designs with glossy patent leather trims and ankle boots featuring crystal-studded maxi buckles—all capturing the very essence of cold-weather decadence.

As I marvelled at the exquisite designs, I couldn't help but feel a resonance between the luxurious footwear and the glamorous atmosphere outside the boutique, where the city itself seemed to mirror the feelings of grandeur.

My visits to Vienna, though frequent, never ceased to bring with them new delights, nestled within mazes of tiny streets with old cobblestone pavements and dotted with small ateliers showcasing modern art. Beyond its renowned cultural heritage and classical music scene, Vienna pulsated with the energy of young, exciting designers eager to make a sartorial statement. In this city, I found myself an avid listener when it came to the waltz of fashion, always attuned to the fresh narratives spun by the creative minds shaping Vienna's contemporary design landscape.

At the top of my must-visit list was Petar Petrov's showroom. Through his designs, Petar Petrov passionately declared that quality is eternally in vogue, and he effortlessly blurred the lines between relaxed and feminine, classic and modern. His creations were exciting; and marked by precision and sharpness. Catering to a clientele that values unparalleled quality, he relied on the trifecta of clean lines, noble materials, and tasteful details.

During my visit, his latest collection showcased a play on proportions, featuring jackets with intentionally overlong sleeves and a predominant focus on oversized denim and leather pieces. In addition to his effortlessly cool ensembles, Petar Petrov showcased a range of feminine silk garments designed to adhere to the contours of the silhouette. My favourite was a stunning white silk number with delicate polka dots.

In one insightful interview, Petrov acknowledged the label of his designs as 'too commercial'. A moniker he embraced. For him, this characterisation is not an insult but an inspiration rooted in the philosophy that the future begins in the present. His purpose is clear: to craft fashion, not art. He firmly identifies himself as a fashion designer rather than an artist, creating garments not for the confines of a museum but for the everyday people.

Petrov believes that even an everyday look has the power to make us feel extraordinary. He marvels at the transformative effect of different outfits on an individual's appearance. Contrary to conventional wisdom, he argues that our everyday wardrobe holds greater significance than the attire we don for special events. He reflects on the paradoxical tendency to splurge on an extravagant dress worn once, if at all, while neglecting to invest in a high-quality tee shirt that provides daily comfort. In essence, Petrov contends that our chosen attire should make us feel spectacular both on special occasions and on ordinary days.

In that same vein, the 'summer body' or 'beach body' trend has always eluded me. Mirrors are a constant presence in my life, and for the better part of the year, the odds are that someone might catch a glimpse of me sans clothing. The concern for the fleeting impressions of beachgoers I might encounter once in my life seems utterly inconsequential.

As I ponder the concept of self-reinvention, a vivid image comes to mind: my relative's wedding. Her lovely dress and decent shoes were overshadowed by a heavy-handed makeup job that transformed her face into that of a porcelain doll. When I struggled to recognise her, she took it as a compliment, exclaiming, 'I know, right?!' with a beaming smile at her over-crafted appearance. I'm sure even the groom had trouble recognising his bride. The question lingers—why transform one's appearance for special occasions or different seasons?

Returning to our Viennese designer, every facet of his latest collection struck a chord with me. What was not to like? The designs erred on the side of caution, avoiding extremes of innovation or antiquity that might prove bothersome. There were no jarring surprises, and the consistent and undeniable quality of each piece was obvious. The craftsmanship was impeccable. Beyond his customary colour palette, the collection featured several pieces with black and white stripes, underscoring the designer's affinity for graphic patterns—hardly a revelation, as I had read about his frequent recourse to Viennese modernism for inspiration.

Browsing a bit more, I discovered a selection of well-tailored, effortlessly chic pieces that I knew would seamlessly integrate into my capsule wardrobe. Their versatility allowed for a wide variety of occasions, be it a casual breakfast with Sophia, a bustling day at work, a haute cuisine dinner with Alessia, or even a Sunday morning church service with my grandmother. Although my attendance at the latter is infrequent, I knew I could confidently showcase Petar Petrov's creations should the occasion arise.

In Vienna, my second stop was Femme Maison, a haven of elegance and simplicity where every piece was meticulously handcrafted within the city's bounds. The minimalist design was not just a stylistic choice; but a commitment to ethical and sustainable fashion, and utilised high-quality fabrics like Austrian wool, silk, and cotton. Femme Maison carves its niche by embracing feminine silhouettes, drawing inspiration from the refinement of 1950s/60s couture. There's a delightful touch of old-school charm reminiscent of Manolo Blahnik, but for garments.

    I loved that the inspiration for their handmade silk gowns drew from the iconic style of the late 1960s and 70s. Particularly, the Helmut Newton portrait immortalising Faye Dunaway enjoying breakfast by the pool the morning after the Oscars. This glamorous yet incredibly intimate moment showcased a powerful woman who triumphed with the most prestigious award in the cinematic world. The setting was a departure from the red carpet and the glamour of the previous night and highlighted the timeless vision of a strong woman in a well-made dress. Even in the morning light, both the dress and the accolade retained their beauty, preserving the magic of the award night.

    My first encounter with Femme Maison's modern yet timeless designs took place at the illustrious Galeries Lafayette in Paris. In my quest for a simple white blazer that didn't lean too heavily towards a corporate aesthetic, I conveyed my preferences to the resident Lafayette assistant. To my surprise, she introduced me to a Femme Maison sleek white blazer—slightly oversized, yet delicately refined.

    Discovering an 'Austrian' brand in the heart of Paris was an unexpected delight. The moment I slipped into that posh piece, I was convinced it was a serendipitous find, and I couldn't pass up the opportunity to bring it home. Every time I put on that blazer, I am met with a cascade of compliments.

    My anticipation for Femme Maison, in its hometown, was set at a high bar. While I encountered unique styles, nothing quite aligned with my wardrobe as harmoniously as that white blazer. Despite leaving the atelier without merely a paper bag in hand, I departed with lasting impressions. The nostalgic storefront exuded a touch of the French Riviera, a hint of Yves Saint Laurent's '70s glamour, and a dash of Old Hollywood charm—all nestled in the heart of Vienna. What Femme Maison and Petar Petrov shared, beyond their commitment to high-quality fabrics and impeccable finishes, was an inclination toward something beyond a fashion revolution. Both brands opted for evolution over revolution—embracing a classic foundation while steadily integrating modern elements.

I, too, was open to evolving... specifically when it came to my private life. Despite being content with my current state, I yearned to take my relationship to the next level and was ready to embrace significant changes. The decision to prioritise my partner and make him the focal point of my life represented a profound shift for me.

So, in Vienna that evening, I chose to momentarily divert from my passion for fashion, redirecting my focus towards my love life. It seemed like a healthier choice for both my heart and wallet. I recall a newspaper article that caught my attention, as my seatmate on the train was engrossed in it. The article covered a consumer expenditure survey in China, suggesting that singles tend to allocate a more substantial portion of their income towards style. Although I refrained from prying into my seatmate's relationship status or borrowing the newspaper to read the article myself, I absorbed the findings, contemplating my own situation. The study classified singles as 'individuals of any age group not currently in a romantic relationship, whether by choice or circumstance.'

As mentioned earlier, dear reader, it was time to prioritise my relationship. I believe it's appropriate for you to get to know Daniel a bit better. Although, I must admit, at that time, around our weekend in Vienna, I hadn't gotten to know him thoroughly myself. However, I did have, at least, a sense of his appearance, and I realise now that I haven't shared any of that with you.

When we talk about love, our initial thoughts often revolve around the remarkable qualities that make our beloved stand out. For me, Daniel was nothing short of extraordinary.

What made him truly remarkable, however, was not just his impressive qualities, but the extraordinary experience of being around him. Unlike the charismatic personalities that command attention in a crowded room, Daniel possessed an understated charm that drew me in. At 1.80 metres tall, he was slightly taller than me, with a slender build that felt like a safe haven. His straight posture and elegant movements exuded confidence and poise. His hair, almost black, and his eyes, deep brown—which may have been common traits, but they held a certain something. I couldn't tell what it was about them. Brown eyes are commonly associated and linked to intelligence and trustworthiness—traits that would take on a nuanced significance in the unfolding of our story.

But what truly set Daniel apart was his voice and the art of his speech. He had an innate ability to forge an instant connection with people, making them feel as if they were the most important person in the world. In a world where we all seek to find the individuality of ourselves, Daniel's certainly resonated in the cadence of his speech.

And as I delved deeper into our connection, my friends were quick to offer their perspectives. Sophia noted his sharp wit while Alessia cryptically remarked that he had 'something'. Their words were measured, leaving much unsaid, but I understood my friends well enough to sense that their initial impressions were not overwhelmingly positive. Nonetheless, my curiosity persisted, and I was aware that their guarded remarks were an attempt to let me explore the connection without undue influence.

Daniel owned a small publishing company and led a life that traversed various locales, primarily driven by his work. Hamburg, he claimed, was his home base. Conversations about his family were sparse, and when probed, he would casually mention a younger brother residing on Sylt. His love for the sea manifested in his summer retreats to a house on the North Sea, equipped with a self-made 'port' where a small boat patiently waited for a passenger. Those sun-soaked days were dedicated to sailing, surfing, and reading, often punctuated by lively gatherings with friends and neighbours. His invitation for me to join his famed summer parties hinted at a future together, though the location—charming yet windswept—didn't quite align with my visions of a southern summer.

The thought of the North Sea's sandy beaches and the promise of cosy reading sessions wrapped in blankets tempered my reservations, however. Besides, the prospect of trying windsurfing kindled a sense of adventure within my soul, something I had been leaning into more frequently.

As I meandered through the maze of narrow streets in Vienna, my mind danced with a cascade of thoughts, each step compounding my anticipation. The city, once again, revealed itself to me as a resplendent masterpiece, with architectural wonders standing tall alongside charming cobblestone alleys. The air was infused with the irresistible aroma of freshly baked pastries, creating an immersive experience that enticed passersby with the promises of Viennese delights. The scent also served as a gentle reminder of my growing hunger, which in turn brought my thoughts back to the imminent dinner with Daniel.

The realisation that I was running behind schedule snapped me back to the urgency of the moment. Amidst the many distractions of Vienna's streets, I quickened my pace, eager to reach the restaurant Daniel had chosen for our evening rendezvous. Upon arrival, the hostess greeted me with a warm smile and guided me to the carefully arranged table where Daniel was sitting. The dining room atmosphere hummed with an undercurrent of excitement, heightened by the subtle clinking of cutlery and the muted laughter of other patrons. The ambient glow of dimmed lights cast a soft halo over the surroundings, and I felt like Daniel had found the most perfect, intimate enclave within the bustling city.

As I approached, Daniel, already immersed in the ambience, looked up from his glass of sparkling wine. His eyes met mine with a familiarity that transcended mere recognition. At that moment, his gaze felt like a comforting embrace that was beckoning me into the shared sanctuary of our evening.

I'm not exactly sure what we devoured that night, but I'm pretty sure it was love. The main courses were mere mortals, mere sustenance for our insatiable appetites, while the real feast was the one he served up with his piercing eyes and devastating smile. Each bite was a revelation, each sip a promise of forever. We laughed, drank, and ate some more. It was as if the world outside had melted away, leaving only the two of us suspended in a timeless bubble of togetherness.

Ugh, that night! Thinking back, it was like a scene straight out of a rom-com—the electricity, the connection, the feeling that anything was possible. Everything felt like the beginning of a beautiful love story, the kind you devour in a single sitting with a box of chocolates. But here's the thing: sometimes fairy tales fizzle out faster than a Cosmo on a hot summer day.

CHAPTER EIGHT

'There are exactly as many special occasions in life as we choose to celebrate,' said the Opera singer Robert Breault.

On that particular evening, I gathered with the girls at the restaurant at the Opera, and we celebrated absolutely nothing. But it didn't feel like nothing. In reality, we had a multitude of reasons to revel in the moment. We were given the invaluable gift of each other's company, the backdrop of our resplendent city, the means to indulge in a four-course dinner at a sophisticated restaurant, premium tickets to Madama Butterfly later that night, the realisation of equal rights with men, the privilege of expressing our opinions freely in the country we called home, and a wardrobe teeming with an array of exquisite shoes. It was a night of gratitude for the countless blessings that were present in our lives.

That evening, I felt like a million bucks, and it wasn't just the champagne. My skin was radiant, like a perfectly toned tan on a summer day. I'd discovered the secret to effortless, glass-like perfection—a whispered magic that only the most skilled makeup artists know. And let me tell you, that gold-dusted wonder was worth every scepticism. It was like wearing a subtle, shimmering veil that made my skin glow from within. The skilled hands at Sandra's salon had bestowed upon me a fresh blow dry, and her fabulous team managed to squeeze me in for a glossy red manicure, adding that final touch of glamour.

My ensemble oozed confidence—a daring red, form-fitting Dolce and Gabbana midi dress crafted in Italy from lustrous satin. The dress was supported by a corset bustier with boning, enhancing my silhouette. Paired with pointy, sheer slingback heels, the getup was nothing short of impeccable.

As I sashayed through the elegant restaurant, the warmth of the staff's hospitality wrapped itself around me like a velvet cloak. The aromatic scent of fine cuisine wafted through the air, tantalising my taste buds and elevating my mood to new heights. We indulged in a bottle of our favourite rosé, and to our delight, another arrived—this time, on the house. It was one of those nights to surrender to the ambience, to let the soft strains of jazz and the gentle clinking of glasses wash over me, and to indulge in the sublime pleasures of life.

A captivating couple strolled into view, their undeniable chemistry adding to the evening's magic. The husband, clearly relishing the attention of three other ladies alongside his very sophisticated companion, started telling us all engaging stories of nights past, transporting us back four decades to the couple's earliest visits to the theatre. On one such occasion, their love story unfolded. She was accompanied by her affluent father, and he was a waiter with a dream bigger than his paycheck (opening his own restaurant). They crossed paths. The next day, she returned alone to see the same show, just to hopefully see him again. They started dating in secret, with him whisking her away to hidden gems in the city where he could afford to treat her to dinner or a glass of wine. These unknown spots became her new favourites, and she cherished his company just as much as the unexpected experiences.

But one concern weighed heavily on her mind: her father's reaction to their relationship. Would he disapprove of a man who didn't fit the mould of her social circle? Yet, her father's response was a delightful surprise. He didn't ask about his social status or education; instead, he embraced their love with open arms. He never interfered in their relationship and even offered his support in building it. His faith in the young man's potential led to the opening of his first restaurant, marking the beginning of a successful career in hospitality. The couple's entrepreneurial ventures continued to flourish, with establishments in their city, Miami, New York, and eventually, a hotel.

As we were reflecting on this remarkable love story, we were reminded that true love doesn't seek to match expectations but rather finds common ground in looking outward together in the same direction.

Amidst the chronicles, when touching upon the sensitive subject of infertility they had faced, his partner tactfully intervened whenever he ventured into overly detailed territory, guiding the conversation away from the darkest corners of their journey. Their playful banter, punctuated by the husband's infectious laughter, left us only wishing to be as lucky as they were—to find someone who will make us laugh, who will make us feel alive.

They were like a perfectly paired cocktail, a sweet and spicy blend that had weathered life's storms and emerged even stronger. Watching them together just reminded me why we all crave those happily ever afters. As we said our goodbyes, it felt like parting from friends rather than strangers we had just met. Yes, connections can be made in the blink of an eyelash, sometimes stronger sometimes than anything you build over years. They'd rekindled a flicker of hope in our cynical hearts, a reminder that love, the real kind, can truly last. And let's be honest, who doesn't need a little faith in forever after every now and then?

Looking back on the first half of the evening, even now, I can't help but think, What a perfect night!

Just moments before the show was set to commence, a sudden wave of nausea swept over me, prompting an urgent dash to the lavatory. Ironically, during this season of my life, I had carefully crafted the perfect look to encounter my ex anytime I left the house, yet the universe seemed determined to orchestrate the worst possible timing. Fate, in its capricious dance, led me to cross paths with him and his date amid the sea of faces at the Opera House later that evening.

In the face of this unexpected encounter, I fumbled through an apology (or, at least, I believe that's what it was) before making a hasty retreat to the bathroom. Inside the sanctuary of an empty stall, I closed the door behind me and found solace in the quiet space. Leaning over the cold toilet seat, my hands instinctively covered my face as a sense of panic set in. The overwhelming emotions stemming from the encounter and the looming fear of staining my satin dress were all too much to handle.

How utterly embarrassing! The thought struck me that he might interpret my sudden retreat as a reaction to him, perhaps assuming I was unnerved by his presence or his date. Yes, he was indeed accompanied by someone. However, I didn't manage to get a good look at her—except for a glimpse of her standout footwear as I rushed past them: white stilettos, patent leather.

In an attempt to regain my composure, I checked my makeup in the restroom mirror, summoning a forced smile to conceal any lingering displeasure. Upon returning to our table, I swiftly requested the bill and implored the girls to be vigilant. Throughout the remainder of the evening, we conducted a discreet search mission, scanning the crowd in the grand hall and keeping a keen eye out for those white patent leather heels during the fifteen-minute intermission.

In the quiet confines of the taxi during our journey home, Alessia broke the extended silence. 'He kinda ruined our night.'

Though I had sensed Sophia's growing annoyance with me, her sudden and direct declaration caught me off guard.

'Actually, Elena ruined it,' she asserted, turning to face me. 'Why do you even care about him? Have you forgotten how unhappy and unworthy he made you feel? Why let him tarnish even a few hours of your day after everything you've been through? He didn't ruin your evening; you did it to yourself. You are a grown-up, super intelligent, stunningly beautiful woman who spent her night with friends at the Opera, searching for a self-centred man who once made you feel average, if not miserable at times. What if we had found him? What would have changed? And even if he has a new girlfriend now, you should feel sorry for her, not jealous.'

I remained silent, absorbing the truth in Sophia's words. She was right, and the weight of her wisdom settled in. I embraced her tightly, then turned to Alessia, who mouthed a sincere I'm sorry. I nodded in acknowledgement, exchanged a cheek kiss with Alessia, and swiftly exited the taxi at my stop.

As I climbed the stairs to the second floor, I reflected on Sophia's words and still attempted to recall the fleeting image of the girl in white patent leather heels... to feel sorry for her, not jealous of her.

Besides, white shoes tiptoe along the fine line between tasteful elegance and potential tackiness. Their devil-may-care impracticality has a certain je ne sais quoi, but let's be real— they're still a bit of a flashy indulgence. In a world that's trying too hard to be polished and perfect, untouched by the imperfections and stains that make life interesting, white shoes stand out as a bold statement—or, as a loud mistake.

When the weekend was over, I had a plan in mind: to diligently comb through our system in search of any customers who might have purchased the specific stilettos that had caught my attention. I considered the possibility that perhaps they were a gift, possibly even from him. But I aimed to put these thoughts on hold until the workweek resumed.

I also hoped that the next day, I would wake up feeling content with myself, indifferent to other people's lives, and forget about the encounter altogether. Determined to shift my focus away from The Surgeon's newfound life and concentrate on my own, I decided on a spontaneous trip to Hamburg to spend the day with Daniel, with plans to return on the first available flight on Monday. That was the strategy. And, in moments when things didn't unfold as anticipated, I reminded myself that everything happens for a reason.

...

Hamburg held a special place in my heart, as not only Daniel's hometown but also the birthplace of two of my all-time favourite fashion designers—each revered for distinct reasons. One captivated me with his unique personality, while the other enamoured me with her sophisticated minimalism.

While I might not be an avid enthusiast of his eponymous label, I held immense respect for Karl Lagerfeld for pushing boundaries during his tenure at Chanel. His impact was evident in the shortened and tightened skirts, elevated heels, and the redefined iconic handbags. Yet, my admiration extended beyond his design strategy; it was fueled by his remarkable personality. His audacity, extravagance, and ferociously creative endeavours defined him as a human. Love him or hate him for his directness and flamboyant lifestyle, he refused to conform and was often labelled as self-centred. To me, he epitomised the art of being unapologetically oneself, honing the cleverness not to take life too seriously. His personality, more vibrant than the colours of his brand or the hues he consistently wore, left a lasting mark on me.

'He is the only person who could make black and white a colour,' Claudia Schiffer once remarked about her friend, who, in her words, *'transformed her from a shy German girl into a supermodel.'* To her, he was akin to magic.

Lagerfeld was truly a unique individual. One particularly amusing yet fascinating detail about him caught my attention: images of Lagerfeld's home library showcased a collection of thousands of books, stacked horizontally rather than conventionally vertically. The rationale behind this unconventional approach, I learned, was to eliminate the need to tilt his head when perusing the titles—a quirk that, upon reflection, made perfect sense.

This distinctive choice, as well as countless others, reflected his preference for doing things differently. It became a fashion statement in its own right, a characteristic move from someone perpetually ahead of the curve in the world of fashion. Interestingly, this trend has now trickled down into the domain of interior design, particularly with fashion and photography coffee table books. I found myself adopting a similar approach at home, initially stacking a few books without much thought about the arrangement, only to continue seeking out and adding new ones on top. It occurred to me that Lagerfeld's journey with his library might have started in a similar manner. Eventually, it likely became impractical to revert to vertical stacking, especially with the weighty photography books in his collection.

Ultimately, Karl Lagerfeld's impact on fashion was not just a result of his designs but also his ingenious ability to turn the ordinary into the extraordinary. Once, in a stroke of brilliance, he transformed a simple couture show into an immersive experience where the runway transcended its conventional role. Models became narrators, each embodying a different character in the grand story that unfolded for the attendees. The catwalk itself transformed into a life-sized library, with shelves laden with books showcasing Lagerfeld's multifaceted creativity.

As models walked through the academic setting, the audience not only saw exquisite garments but also witnessed a story told through fashion. The collection itself was a fusion of classic elegance and Lagerfeld's avant-garde vision, seamlessly blending the worlds of literature and couture. Lagerfeld built his career on unparalleled originality and was successful in pushing the boundaries of what a fashion show could be. His unique approach elevated fashion to an art form, leaving an indelible mark on the industry.

Another compelling fashion combination of contemporary design and timeless refinement is what makes Jil Sander my favourite German designer. Like a perfectly crafted Manolo Blahnik, her style is both seductive and understated. And yet, it's her unwavering dedication to her vision, that daredevil spirit of hers, that truly sets her apart. At the tender age of 24, she traded in her trusty steed (or, rather, her car) for a chance at stardom and took a bold leap of faith by securing a loan from the bank.

Jil Sander, a pioneer in defying societal norms, was an advocate for the beauty and comfort of pants, particularly jeans —a bold choice that challenged the constraints of women's fashion during times when women had to ask their husbands if they could work, or if they could get a driver's licence. Undeterred in her goal to give women the power that men knew, she donned her jeans and embarked on the journey to establish a fashion brand in Hamburg. Armed with her mother's old sewing machine, she set to work on new garments, laying the foundation for an international brand that aimed to blend sophistication, modernity, and comfort. The bold German designer reshaped men's functional clothing into delicate pieces tailored for the emerging cadre of confident women assuming executive roles during the early 1980s. Her high-end fashion designs struck a perfect balance between wearability and sensuality, continuously challenging traditional norms.

Her achievements didn't stop there. Jil Sander ventured into the skincare market, expanding her influence and leaving her signature mark on the beauty industry. Notably, she launched the highly successful Jil Sander perfume, securing the fourth position in West Germany's sales ranking, trailing only behind giants like Estée Lauder, Lancôme, and Chanel. Jil Sander's legacy is not just a tale of fashion; it's an inspiring narrative of courage, innovation, and the unwavering pursuit of dreams. Legend has it that during the early days of her eponymous brand, she would carefully inspect the pieces displayed in her boutique each morning. One day, as she examined a rack of impeccably tailored suits, she noticed a subtle deviation in the alignment of the buttons on one jacket.

Famously detail-oriented, Sander summoned her team to address the issue. However, upon closer inspection, it turned out that the misaligned buttons were not a flaw but a deliberate design choice by one of her designers, who was known to be somewhat experimental. Rather than dismissing the stylistic departure, Jil Sander—known for her openness to innovation—embraced the unconventional detail, allowing it to remain.

Even in the pursuit of minimalism, Jil Sander has always been willing to appreciate and integrate unexpected elements. It is anecdotes like these that reflect her unique blend of exacting standards and forward-thinking approach, making Jil Sander a trailblazer in the world of fashion. She is more a textile engineer than a designer. For her, structure and sculpture are everything. Another anecdote says that she would fit garments on the mannequins, and someone else would come afterwards to do the drawings.

While Jil Sander is no longer directly involved with her brand, the label has admirably remained true to Jil's vision of sensual simplicity by consistently adhering to a refined colour palette featuring black, grey, white, beige, brown, and dark blue. In 1997, they introduced the groundbreaking concept of essential luxury to men's fashion, a vision they have steadfastly upheld throughout the years. Jil Sander's lasting impact remains a significant force in shaping the fashion landscape, making her an icon of feminism yesterday and today.

CHAPTER NINE

I was intent on surprising him. Fortunately, I was also armed with the address gleaned from the shipping document that accompanied a tea maker and original teas from Hamburg he once sent me. Feeling thoroughly prepared, I set out to accomplish what I deemed a romantic gesture. It wasn't my first impromptu visit to a man's apartment, but this time, the stakes were higher—I knew him, but he had no inkling of my imminent arrival.

Despite my confidence that he would appreciate the surprise, a nagging fear lingered. What if my actions leaned more toward stalker-like rather than romantic? The address I sourced from the shipping document might well belong to his office rather than his home, and I could find myself awkwardly knocking on the front door of a business on a quiet Sunday.

Opting for a more cautious approach, I decided to text him the moment my plane touched down in Hamburg.

(Me) I just landed in Hamburg. Heading to Bussestrasse :)
(Daniel) ???
(Daniel) Are you joking?
(Daniel) I am not at home.
(Daniel) How do you know my address?
(Daniel) Are you serious?
(Me) No worries. Should I wait for you at yours or come where you are? I packed light; I just have hand luggage.

His response, or rather lack thereof, fueled my growing uncertainty. Twenty minutes passed, and as I contemplated searching for the next available flight back home, my phone finally rang—it was Daniel calling.

'Where are you?' His tone was urgent, cutting through the bustling noise of the airport.

'At the airport,' I maintained a steady response, though the ambient sounds of the terminal, combined with the tension in his voice, resembled the chaotic energy of a sports arena.

'You can't be serious! Why would you come here without telling me?' He was definitely upset. Oh yes.

'I thought I would surprise you. Now I see that I was successful,' my voice trailed off as I realised my attempt at humour carried a tinge of regret.

'How do you know my address?' He asked again.

'Why are you so upset?' I responded to his question with my own.

'Have you been stalking me?' His accusation, sharper this time, cut through the airport's constant hum. I had heard him loud and clear.

Once again, I attempted a light-hearted remark, desperately trying to use humour to cool the blazing heat of his words. 'I thought we were in a relationship. I know the addresses of all of my exes...'

It felt as if, right there in the midst of the Hamburg Airport, he was on the brink of joining the ranks of those exes. We began at an airport, and it seemed cosmically hilarious that we might be parting ways at one. Except, this time, I was here at the airport alone, while he remained elusive in Bussestrasse or some other undisclosed location.

A veil of secrecy shrouded each of his responses, leaving me apprehensive about what revelations might be hiding under the surface. The weekend had already taken a turn for the worse, and a disconcerting feeling settled in the pit of my stomach.

'I'll call you in ten minutes,' he said and hung up.

Ten minutes too late. In that span, I navigated my way to the Lufthansa counter, securing tickets for a Munich-bound flight departing in just two hours. I contemplated the prospect of spending the day in Hamburg, relishing the vibrant atmosphere on my own. The city was large enough for our paths not to cross inadvertently, that I was sure of. Yet, apprehension lingered; and the risk—albeit miniscule—of a chance encounter remained.

Looking down at my boarding pass, several thoughts quickly dashed through my mind. What if he does call me back? What if this was all some big misunderstanding? Maybe he was having a difficult day. Maybe he wants to talk about it when he picks me up from the airport. Maybe I should stay and wait for him.

I was terrified to be left with these thoughts for even a moment longer. The potential for a change of heart was present, and I knew I needed to stamp it out. Suddenly, I found myself retracing my steps. As if I wasn't controlling my own body, I returned to the airline counter and swiftly obtained tickets for a Stockholm-bound plane that was on the verge of boarding. After all, I was already at the airport. The dilemma hung in the air: should I return home and succumb to tears or seize the opportunity to fly to Stockholm and celebrate life? Stockholm was one of my favourite fashion cities, and I had a close friend who recently relocated there to work for Acne Studios. I called her.

'Of course, you should come to my place,' Livia exclaimed excitedly over the phone. 'I have this gorgeous two-bedroom apartment in the heart of the city, all to myself since my flatmate is launching her first line of flip-flops in Hawaii.'

Intrigued by the mention of Hawaii and the flip-flops, I boarded the plane to Stockholm and felt confident in my decision to pivot my plans. I hailed a taxi and headed to the address Livia shared via WhatsApp. The vehicle came to a halt in front of a narrow, four-story structure. Its architecture, aged and intricate, hinted at

Rococo influences with its curvy lines, though the recent renovations made it feel contemporary. The top floor stood out, appearing as if it had been added later, with a design aesthetic markedly distinct from the rest. Livia emerged on the balcony of that upper level, waving enthusiastically and shouting down to me, 'Elena, fourth floor!'

Her signature scent welcomed me at the entrance, a delicate blend of jasmine and vanilla that was unmistakably hers. As I entered Livia's apartment, I was immediately captivated by the harmonious blend of modern aesthetics and vintage charm. The two-bedroom haven was a masterclass in stylish minimalism. In true Stockholm fashion, the living room showcased contemporary furniture with plush cushions in natural hues, juxtaposed against exposed brick walls that retained a whisper of the building's history. Large windows flooded the space with natural light, offering a panoramic view of Stockholm. I took a deep breath as I looked across the picturesque cityscape.

Livia's taste in decor showcased an eclectic fusion of styles, combining sleek Scandinavian designs with carefully curated, maximalist vintage pieces. Black and white photos leaned on the windows, complementing the dark hardwood floors that gracefully stretched across the living area. Potted plants were scattered across every possible corner, and I remembered that my friend has had a green thumb for as long as I could remember.

As I marvelled at the space, Livia, with her effervescent energy, shared more details about her roommate's aforementioned flip-flop business. We settled in the stylish kitchen.

'Sounds like fun!' I exclaimed as I perched on a high bar chair, ready to distract myself with the many stories Livia always had to share.

'But you don't sound like fun. What's wrong?' she astutely observed, sensing a hint of melancholy in my demeanour.

'Long story,' I muttered, signalling my reluctance to reveal the complexities of my emotions.

As she acknowledged my unspoken boundaries with a nod of understanding, Livia's eyes gracefully traced the delicate contours of the beautiful bouquet of flowers I had procured on the way. I asked the taxi driver to make a stop at a charming little flower shop, and I had picked up her favourite blooms: white peonies.

A warm smile engulfed her lips as she uttered, 'My favourite.'

Back in Munich, Livia purchased white peonies for herself all the time, so I was confident in my selection for her. I also suspected that along with bringing her bubbly personality all the way to Sweden, she had also transported her cherished collection of vases to her new flat.

As it turned out, I was right. Livia carefully arranged the peonies in a crystal-glass vase with an aquamarine blue hue, placing the display on the marble countertop in the kitchen.

I noticed that the apartment, bathed in natural light through its expansive windows, displayed a unique design — walls were a rarity, confined only to the single bathroom. Livia and her roommate each had their own beautifully appointed bedrooms, a symphony of individual design tastes that converged within the shared dressing room that sparked a thousand questions in my curious mind.

'I would never wear her clothes, and she would never wear mine. We are poles apart in our styles,' Livia said, motioning to her roommate's clothing rack. 'Plus, even if there was something I could envision wearing, I make it a habit not to dress myself in someone else's clothes. There are so many second-hand shops here in Stockholm, but I always pass by without venturing in. I might spot something interesting and even make a purchase, but deep down, I know I'll never wear it,' Livia explained.

'Even a bag?' I probed, testing the limits of her fashion principles.

'Even a car, my dear,' she responded with a playful smirk. 'So, my flatmate's clothes are untouched territory, and she's well aware that if she borrows something from me, it's a one-time affair. I'm sure she thinks I'm weird, but she's also probably relieved that her wardrobe will remain intact while she's away.'

'Well, I didn't know that about you,' I said, genuinely surprised. 'Considering you're in Sweden and immersed in the world of fashion, I assumed you have an environmentally conscious and re-use mindset.'

'I do. I just re-use my own clothes. I prioritise high-quality pieces and refrain from excessive purchases. The reality is, if I want to maintain this stunning apartment, unrestricted consumerism has to take a backseat,' she chuckled, offering a glimpse into the pragmatic side of her fashion philosophy.

A set of double doors from the kitchen unveiled the entrance to an unexpectedly expansive balcony perched atop the old building, a secret haven with breathtaking views. Livia, with palpable pride, explained that the true magic of the space unfolded in the evening when the balcony and city lights collaboratively illuminated the surroundings. I knew she loved to entertain, and this balcony was just what she needed. Throughout the year, they had transformed it into a living room of sorts. Nestled on this charming terrace was carefully arranged, cosy patio furniture, which encircled an inviting outdoor fireplace. Strategically placed on each side were outdoor heat lamps, promising a comfortable, almost cocoon-like retreat during the colder winter months.

'I don't have to work today, but do you want me to show you my office and the store?' Livia inquired.

'I thought you'd never ask,' I replied, eager to explore the other facets of the vibrant Swedish lifestyle.

I seized my bag and wrapped my scarf tightly, briskly making my way into the enchanting world of Acne Studios. Thankfully, I packed my small suitcase in anticipation of the capricious winds in Hamburg. It held all the essentials for a city equally known for its erratic weather—Stockholm. However, I realised that the carefully selected array of enticing lingerie I had packed might find itself untouched throughout the weekend.

Acne stands for 'Ambition to Create Novel Expressions'—though originally, it was called 'Associated Computer Nerd Enterprises'. I guess the initial term reflects the company's quirky sense of humour. Jonny Johansson, the founder, had already cut his teeth at Diesel before deciding to pen his own fashion story. Knowing a thing or two about making jeans, he launched Acne Studios with a clever P.R. campaign: creating about a hundred pairs of narrow-cut unisex jeans with red seams and giving them away to friends, family, and clients. Through a friend of a friend—because, let's face it, connections are everything—those limited-edition jeans found their way into the pages of Swedish ELLE. And from ELLE, they finally made the leap to retailer shelves. It just goes to show that in the world of fashion, a little ambition and a lot of creativity can turn a simple pair of jeans into a worldwide sensation.

Jeans served as the foundational cornerstone for Acne Studios, a legacy that endures to this day. The brand's identity further extends to embrace oversized leather jackets, a distinctive signature that has captivated attention and admiration alike. Johansson, the creative force propelling Acne Studios, revels in the art of playing with proportions, often affirming, 'Proportion is always more interesting than decoration.' This design philosophy has materialised in a diverse array of fashion statements, spanning from voluminous jackets and sweaters to cropped tops, shorts, and high-waisted trousers, each bearing the unmistakable imprint of the brand. Celebrating nearly three decades of creative ingenuity, Acne Studios continues to define itself as an influential presence in the global fashion landscape. Its reach spans a network of boutiques in various countries, speaking to Acne's inherently global appeal. Livia, a discerning fashion connoisseur, frequently bragged about the brand's creative prowess. She talked about Acne Studios not as her place of work but as an incubator where innovation and artistic expression thrive in unison. From my perspective, it sounded like the perfect place for my friend to build her career.

Their entire ethos revolved around self-expression, embodied by the founder's proclamation that they sell an emotional experience more than they sell clothes. I have always subscribed to this belief system; when we think of fashion, the significance should lie not only in the items we purchase but in how these acquisitions evoke feelings within us. Acne gets it — we want clothes that make us feel fabulous. Clothes that tell our story.

And speaking of narratives, remember that red silk Valentino dress I snagged in Rome? It was the first time a man had chosen a dress for me. Unfortunately, the guy didn't stick around, but the dress? That was a forever kind of love. It hung proudly in my closet, a reminder of a past adventure. It would be quite bizarre if it were the other way around — the man lingering in my closet while the dress didn't make the cut. After all, a high-quality silk dress like that deserves its happily ever after, even if the date didn't end that way.

As I learned more about the essence of Acne Studios, I turned to Livia, seeking a singular word to encapsulate its spirit. Without hesitation, she declared: cool. And she was right. The brand quickly became synonymous with a chic and effortlessly stylish vibe and was worn in cities across the globe by 'cool girls' who threw a funky scarf over a basic sweatshirt and somehow looked like they walked off the runway. Acne Studios has carved a distinctive niche for itself in the fashion landscape, elevating coolness from a descriptor to an intrinsic aspect of its identity.

The Swedes have always been conscious of their fashion choices. Forget fleeting trends—they're all about timeless style with a sustainable twist (because saving the planet is always in fashion). Their style whispers volumes. We're talking a deep denim devotion, a vintage eye that could spot a Chanel bag from a mile away, and an unshattered commitment to quality.
Every outfit you see, whether it's a head-turning look from Acne or a quirky vintage score, tells a story. And let me tell you, these stories are good! Maybe it's because the weather in Stockholm is like a bad ex; unpredictable and keeps you on your toes. So naturally, the Swedes are layering experts, masters at throwing on clothes that can be easily peeled off or piled on depending on the hour. Clean lines, oversized silhouettes—it's all about minimalism with a major dose of chic. Every piece has a purpose, designed to look fabulous while making it easy to navigate those bustling city streets, whether you're strutting your stuff on foot or cruising by on a bicycle. Because who needs cabs and carbon emissions when you've got two wheels and killer style?

And Livia? Let's just say she's the epitome of Swedish style done right. This girl seamlessly blended her unique personality with the Stockholm fashion scene. Effortlessly chic and ridiculously practical, she wasn't just part of the crowd; she was a showstopper in her own right. Basically, the epitome of a Carrie Bradshaw on the streets of Stockholm. That Saturday, she wore a long camel coat that was massively, yet intentionally, oversized. Underneath, she had on a strapless white top tucked into the dreamiest high-waisted jeans you've ever seen. These weren't your average skinny jeans—oh no, these were wide-leg wonders that added a touch of drama with every step she took. Her accessories were minimal but impactful. Delicate gold hoops grazed her ears, and a thin gold necklace peeked out from under her perfectly tousled waves. She carried a mini shoulder bag from Acne Studios in a soft apricot-orange suede. It was the perfect size for her essentials, with a secret weapon on the backside: a hidden mirror for those all-important touch-ups on the go. On her feet, half-covered by the wide-leg jeans, she sported white Adidas sneakers, because in that city, style included a level of practicality. Her makeup gave away just a hint of natural glam, enough to highlight her gorgeous features without going overboard. Let's be honest; this girl woke up like this—effortlessly chic and ready to take the city by storm.

After a half-hour of riveting conversation about Acne, Livia led me out of the store. We wandered through the quaintly narrow streets of Stockholm, and although they were not her taste, Livia showed me the hidden gems of the city—the second-hand vintage stores. Tucked away like well-kept secrets, these quaint boutiques contained a treasure trove of clothing items that had all lived their own, full lives before being consigned. I had always viewed vintage as a living narrative, each piece carrying with it the imprints of its previous owner. As we walked into the first shop, the aroma of aged leather and the faint rustle of silk skirts hung in the air.

'Isn't this place charming?' Livia asked as she sifted through a rack of floral dresses.

'It's like stepping into a time capsule,' I replied, running my fingers over the intricate beadwork on a 1920s flapper dress. 'Every piece has so much history.'

Livia smiled, pulling out a perfectly preserved leather jacket. 'This one probably saw some wild nights.'

We laughed, imagining the jacket on a rebellious teenager in the seventies, sneaking into concerts and living life on the edge. Each item we picked up seemed to whisper its memories to us, from the delicate lace gloves to the bold, patterned scarves.

As we continued exploring, Livia shared anecdotes about her own fashion adventures. 'I once found the most incredible pair of vintage Chanel shoes in a tiny shop just like this. They were my size, can you believe it? It was like they were waiting for me.'

'That's the magic of vintage,' I said. 'It's as if the clothes find you, rather than the other way around.'

'I never wore them, though. But I still have them. I know we're the same size. I can show them to you once we're back at the apartment.'

'Thanks, Livi. I don't mind second-hand, but I draw the line at shoes. Everyone has their own posture and walk—it just doesn't feel right.'

We moved to another section of the store, where a wall of handbags caught my eye. 'Look at this one,' I exclaimed, holding up a beaded clutch. 'It's like a piece of art.'

Livia nodded. 'Exactly. And unlike fast fashion, these pieces were made to last. They've already stood the test of time.'

We spent hours in those shops, each discovery more exciting than the last. And the excitement did not come from the clothes and accessories on their own; it was because of the stories they carried and the joy of uncovering them together. By the time we left, my arms were full of unique finds, and my heart was a little fuller too.

Walking back through the cobblestone streets, I couldn't help but feel a deep appreciation for this city and its hidden treasures. 'Thanks for sharing this with me, Liv,' I said.

'Anytime,' she replied, her smile warm and genuine. 'Stockholm has a lot more secrets to reveal. We've only just begun.'

In the heart of Stockholm, the ritual of fika reigns supreme. Swedes, aficionados of this sacred coffee break, have filled Stockholm with a plethora of charming cafés, each offering its own take on the perfect cup of joe. As my arms grew weary from the weight of shopping bags laden with newfound treasures, Livia and I sought refuge in one such intimate haven —a cosy café that dampened the noise of the city's hustle. The comforting aroma of freshly brewed coffee greeted us as we entered and spotted a free table by the window. The fatigue from our shopping spree quickly dissipated as we settled into the plush chairs. Amidst the inviting atmosphere, we indulged in the ritual of fika. Or, in our version of it. Instead of the house coffee, we sipped imported rosé, savoured homemade bread and oil while waiting for our meal, and shared stories. Opting for a healthy lunch, I surrendered to the culinary prowess of the chef, indulging in a symphony of flavours meticulously crafted into a vibrant salad. The plate resembled an art canvas, adorned with fresh, locally sourced ingredients that danced in perfect symphony—a medley of crisp greens, succulent heirloom tomatoes, and avocados kissed by the Nordic sun (or maybe the Netherlands?! as the largest avocado supplier to Sweden).

'Isn't this just perfect? I missed you, girl.' Livia mused, clinking my glass.

Though I hadn't probed, in a heartfelt moment, Livia felt compelled to share a sentiment with me. 'I find contentment here in Stockholm. Mostly. I mean, you also experience joy in Munich on certain days… and perhaps feel a bit out of sorts on others. It's less about the city itself and more a reflection of our internal states. We are the architects of our joy, not the cityscape, the apartment, or the people around us. Happiness is a choice we make for ourselves. If we embrace it, joy becomes our companion. If not, nothing external can rescue or guide us,' my friend, a philosopher disguised as an architect on paper, eloquently articulated.

'Here's to the philosophy that happiness is a choice,' I raised a glass in agreement, toasting to any and every opportunity to indulge in a drink. It was a small but necessary consolation after my unlucky night in Munich and the unfortunate morning in Hamburg.

Our glasses, whether seen as half empty or half full, swirled within it the delicate blush of French rosé. We vowed to create more memories and commit to seeing each other more often. In a mere fortnight, the tables would turn, and Livia would be the one making her way to Munich for Alessia's grand opening celebration. If not sooner, we'd definitely be reunited in time for the festivities.

Our first run-in with Livia happened over a decade ago at a lively student party in Munich. In those days, she was already immersed in the world of architecture while I navigated the final year of my finance studies. During the summer break, Livia pivoted to retail, working at Zara. Post-graduation, she formally transitioned into the store manager role. A few years later, she found herself steering the ship as a Director of Luxury Retail at the esteemed Loro Piana.

Eventually, our paths diverged, and we inadvertently lost contact—for no particular reason, just the natural ebb and flow of young professionals' existence. The universe, in its mysterious ways, decided to reunite us at the Loro Piana boutique when a familiar voice asked if I needed assistance. Joyfully surprised, we reconnected, seizing the opportunity to catch up over dinner that very same evening. It was during this reunion that Livia shared the exciting news of a new role being offered to her at The Shoe Store. Surprisingly, she wasn't enticed by the offer, as she had decided to pursue her long-held dream of completing her architecture degree and venturing into entrepreneurship.

She must have seen my eyes light up at the mention of the store because she quickly inquired if I would be interested in the role originally extended to her and expressed her willingness to introduce me to her connection. At the time, my career plan involved navigating the world of finance within a startup bank — an environment where I found myself the outsider among colleagues with shared interests such as mortgages or mitigation strategies. The contrast was stark, and not long after that, I officially bid adieu to that chapter.

The transition to my new role only further illuminated the profound contrast between my previous job and the newfound joy I discovered at the store. From the very inception, I felt a deep connection to the work at hand, and for this professional bliss, I owed a debt of gratitude to Livia.

However, for Livia, the journey didn't unfold as smoothly as she had envisioned. Despite her passion, boundless ideas, and unwavering motivation, the entrepreneurial path proved to be a challenging plunge into icy waters. Even the warmth of her fervour couldn't thaw the harsh reality — she lacked the requisite experience to dive head-first into entrepreneurship at such a young age. Undeterred, she made a pragmatic decision: to secure a position as a junior architect, gain valuable experience from experts in her field, and then revisit the aspirations to start her own business.

The narrative took yet another twist with the arrival of the cool Swedes and the job opportunity at Acne. Once again, Livia found herself compelled to put her architectural pursuits on hold in favour of this unexpected opportunity. Whether this diversion would prove to be for the better or worse remained an uncertainty at the time. But now, it was clear. I could sense the genuine joy my dear friend derived from her new home and career and the happiness that radiated from within her.

We laughed nearly the entire walk back home, trading stories of our rebellious late-teenage years together. As we walked through her entryway, I was suddenly grateful to have enjoyed an entire afternoon and evening without thinking about the reason why I ended up in Stockholm in the first place. Obviously, those thoughts came flooding back, as they always do. But I was determined not to cast a shadow on our first Swedish weekend together. Her narrative was one of fulfilment, while mine, at that moment, felt like a puzzle, missing a few crucial pieces.

In the inviting ambience of her rooftop apartment, where warm lighting drenched the exposed brick walls and stories of shared wardrobes and flip-flop successes resonated, I hesitated to introduce the uncertainties of my own journey. In some corner of my consciousness, I clung to the hope that my flight to Hamburg the day before was a surreal dream.

...

My weekend, akin to the Swedes, transpired with a certain coolness. Ultimately, the journey mattered more than the starting point, and it was the concluding moments that etched themselves into my memory… for better or for worse.
Throughout the weekend, my phone remained on silent, a deliberate act of detachment from the constant stream of calls and messages. The notifications accumulated, nonetheless. It was only on the return flight that I decided to reveal the messages. And there were quite a few of them.
(Daniel) I am in front of your door.
(Daniel) I'm sorry.
(Daniel) Let's talk.
(Daniel) Where are you?
(Daniel) ???
(Daniel) Do you want me to leave?
(Daniel) Elena, I'm sorry…
(Daniel) Okay.
(Daniel) I am leaving now.
(Daniel) I'll be at The Charles if you want to see me.

(Daniel) Are you coming? Please.
(Daniel) Okay, leaving now...
(Daniel) ?
(Daniel) Please...
(Daniel) I am so sorry.
(Daniel) I'll do anything.
(Daniel) I have to see you.
(Daniel) I can explain.

I set my phone face down and took a deep breath. Despite the avalanche of messages from Daniel pleading for a chance to explain, my weekend had been a delightful escape that I thoroughly enjoyed. I shared wonderful moments with Livia—enjoying a leisurely city stroll, snagging a stylish jacket from Acne Studios with Livia's generous discount (thanks again, Liv), eating good food, and drinking good wine. But now, it was time to confront reality. The air was charged with anticipation as I typed my response.

(Me) Okay. Please explain.

CHAPTER TEN

Returning to my comfort zone felt reassuring after a turbulent weekend.

'Oh, yes, it was the wind. We also had unpleasant turbulence on the flight back last night,' Javier responded, mistakenly linking my comment to the flight.

I didn't get into the details, as time was limited. Shifting the conversation's focus, I inquired about the new collection, anticipating Javier's customary one-word response: gorgeous.

The mood in the boutique buzzed with excitement as the Shoes, Sunset, Sushi event loomed on the horizon. Invitations had been hand-delivered to loyal, esteemed customers, promising an evening of poshness, culinary delights, and the unveiling of our latest collection. In the midst of orchestrating the final details, I found myself intoxicated by the hustle, manoeuvring boxes and ensuring every element was in place for the grand affair.

I scanned the entire floor, triple-checking that nothing was out of order. As my eyes traced the red carpet extended before the counter, my attention was immediately drawn to a distinctive pair of shoes. White patent leather stilettos, pointed and poised, stood out boldly. In the U.S., tradition discourages wearing white shoes after Labor Day, the first Monday in September. However, this was Munich, and there they were—those familiar white stilettos. Instinctively, my spine straightened up, though my gaze was still directed downward. At that moment, the identity of the wearer became apparent... I never forget a pair of shoes. It was his date. Slowly—almost reluctantly—my eyes travelled up to meet hers.

His date was Veronica.

...

We often make the mistake of comparing ourselves to an old lover's new partners. But is this truly necessary in the process of getting over someone? Should we allow ourselves to feel defeated or inadequate if we deem them more physically attractive or accomplished? Or could we choose to take it as a backhanded compliment instead?

After all, this new person was chosen by someone who once found us captivating enough to love. Their taste and standards haven't just changed overnight. By embracing this perspective, the act of comparison can be transformed from a self-punishing exercise into a positive affirmation of our own qualities - both inside and out.

The truth is, the reasons someone falls for a new partner rarely have to do with erasing or replacing their previous love. More likely, it stems from a desire for novelty, new experiences, or unconscious attempts to work through lingering fears or insecurities. The comparisons we make say more about our own insecurities than anyone else's worth.

So rather than torturing ourselves, why not see this new person as evidence that our former love still has excellent taste in partners?

Veronica remained oblivious to my presence, or maybe she was well aware. Could it be that she visited the boutique regularly and asked about my weekend plans as a subtle way of acknowledging my connection to The Surgeon? Or maybe she simply had great taste and was being polite. Regardless, what was there for her to be aware of, anyway? I didn't leave any significant mark on The Surgeon's life. I wasn't in any of the old photos in his apartment. I wasn't the one that used to play that piano in his library. I wasn't the one who helped him decorate... or choose any of the furniture. I just wasn't the one. I couldn't help but wonder, was she the one? She was amazing, and I wished her the best. But I also wished her 'best' wasn't with him.

...

Sophia was getting to know the Englishman better. His name was Giorgio. When the conversation shifted to their past relationships, he dropped a bombshell, revealing that his last relationship lasted for almost twenty years.

'Twenty years! It's like a marriage with children of a legal age!' Sophia exclaimed with widened eyes.

My curiosity piqued, 'Well, did they have any children?'

'He says no,' she replied, uncertainty clouding her tone as she furrowed her brow.

My investigative nature kicked in, and I probed further, 'What did he say? Why did they break up?'

Sophia responded, 'Oh, I would never ask that, Elena. What's the point in asking anyway? He'll just say what I want to hear or what he wants to tell me. One can never know what the truth is. And if he does tell the truth, it will still only be his perspective on the exact story.'

She had a point. 'Sure, but if you don't ask, you will never know.'

'No, Elena, I will never know either way. I didn't even want to know that his last relationship lasted twenty years. I want to know less, not more,' Sophia explained. After a long pause, she added, 'How can I find her? The ex.'

I was surprised, but as a woman, I could empathise with her perspective. 'Why do you want to find her? I thought you wanted to know less, not more.'

'Yes, I did say that... but now I'm dying to see what she's like,' Sophia admitted with a big smile, crossing her hands by her chin.

I refrained from asking why. Sometimes, the actions driven by love defy logical explanations. If Sophia believed she should find the ex, there was only one thing I could say to my friend.

'Let's find the ex.'

...

Daniel made numerous attempts to reach out, emphasising that a message couldn't capture everything he needed to express.
That weekend's events remained shrouded in mystery, leaving me with an uneasy feeling. Alessia's words echoed in my mind — appearances can be deceiving, often shaped by our perceptions rather than reality. Despite my unease, I granted him an opportunity to explain. We arranged to meet at the bar in The Charles on Thursday.

As he sat before me, Daniel seemed different, or perhaps I was viewing him through altered eyes. The remnants of a couple of drinks, likely whiskey, were sprawled out on the table. Opting for water, I signalled the bartender while Daniel motioned for another round. I could tell he was upset, but the sight was somewhat pitiful.

A prolonged silence lingered, creating an almost unbearable tension, and I actually considered leaving. Eventually, Daniel broke the silence, repeating the same apologies I read over text. For a moment, it seemed that would be the extent of our conversation. But it's never that simple.

His voice shaking, he disclosed having a girlfriend with whom he lived. While my intuition had sensed the presence of someone else, the confirmation still sent shockwaves through my heart. He detailed years of being with her, unable to find the opportune moment to end the relationship. Daniel admitted feeling content until our paths crossed, which caused him to grapple with the underlying discontent within his current partnership. Meeting me highlighted the misery he felt, he described. In an attempt to console me, he assured me that I shouldn't carry guilt for disrupting their dynamic, but rather, he expressed gratitude for helping him realise that a relationship could be more than just tolerable.

Should I have harboured guilt? I certainly didn't feel guilty. Ignorance shielded me from knowledge. When we first crossed paths at the London airport, he appeared to be an intelligent, charming, and unattached individual, drawing me in with a whirlwind of affection over the subsequent weeks and months. Little did I know that the façade of the perfect single man would crumble. Once the revelation surfaced about his relationship, my moral compass caused me to question my continued involvement. If I persisted in our connection after discovering his non-single status, perhaps guilt was warranted. Did I really want to carry that?

I slipped a twenty-euro note beneath his emptied glass, declaring the next round was my treat. With my vintage 2.55 in hand, I departed, uncertain whether I wished for him to chase after me, yet still expecting it. Surprisingly, he didn't.

Eight blocks later, upon reaching home, there he stood. He explained that he called a taxi, intending to grant me space on my walk to process the news, acknowledging its less-than-ideal nature.

'We are exceptional together. I love you,' he tightened his grip on my hand, his eyes seeking reassurance. 'Do you love me?'

I hesitated, suddenly feeling the weight of confusion, heartbreak, and... there it was–guilt. 'I don't trust you. I can't trust you. And I can't love you. I'm sorry,' I expressed, hearing my words carry a blend of regret and firmness.

His response was a sombre acknowledgement, 'No, I am sorry.'

'You should be,' I asserted; my tone was firm, but it betrayed a hint of hurt and disappointment.

In a desperate attempt to salvage the situation, he implored, 'I'll leave her. It is not working anyway.'

I was losing patience. 'No, this is not working.'

Pulling my hand away, I reached into my bag for the keys, the tension in the air palpable. As I opened the door, I could still feel him staring in my direction. Emboldened by a false sense of hope, he asked if he could come up with me.

'Six days ago, I realised I didn't know you. I see now that you clearly don't know me either,' I chuckled, unable to fully comprehend his thought process. 'If you knew who I was as a woman, you wouldn't have just asked me that.'

I stepped into the house, and a sense of conviction enveloped me from the words I had spoken. But an air of uncertainty lingered, and I was unsure if he truly comprehended the finality of our situation. Without thinking, I turned back and informed him that he would never hear from me again, and I expected the same treatment. It was then, for the first time that evening, that our eyes met, and I recognised the gaze I had once loved. My expression softened. I found myself not placing blame on him but on the ill-fated timing that had entwined our paths. I understood it was time to close the door of my home before risking the vulnerability of reopening my heart.

...

I was incredulous when Sophia confessed that she had spent the entire morning perusing Giorgio's Instagram followers in the office. Such dedication was uncharacteristic, especially for someone as busy as Sophia. Yet, she had devised a plan. First, she scrutinised each one of his posts, roughly 50 in total. The majority of them featured photos of modern sofas, retro armchairs, Marmor tables, walls with mouldings, painted ceilings, and extravagant paintings, providing a curated glimpse into his aesthetic preferences. A few snapshots captured him in various locations, from L.A. and New York to Monte Carlo. One particular image showcased him in a luxuriant bathrobe, which Sophia reluctantly approved of. I couldn't blame her; it looked like a plush robe.

The highlight of her investigation, however, was a solitary photo featuring a woman seated in an Eames Chair in what seemed to be an opulent hotel lobby. Sophia tapped on the image, but alas, there was no tag to reveal the woman's identity. She was admittedly chic, appearing slightly older than him, though Sophia acknowledged that lighting, a bad hair day, or other factors could distort one's visual age in a photo. Despite the thorough examination, there were no comments under the picture, only a modest count of twenty-something likes.

With a sigh of mild disappointment, Sophia concluded her initial investigation, finding nothing particularly captivating in her search. As she continued scrolling through his profile, the specific information she sought was nowhere to be found. She did, however, find some decent interior design inspiration.

Of course, Sophia was undeterred. She adjusted her strategy, looking into the profiles of individuals he was following —a noticeably shorter list compared to his extensive list of followers. In her logical deduction, the expectation arose that, given their enduring two-decade-long relationship, there would be a substantial overlap in their social circles, perhaps even an entirety of mutual friends. The prospect of discovering shared connections added a layer of intrigue to her ongoing quest for insights. It was conceivable that his ex still followed him, unless something really unsavoury had occurred between them. Sophia combed through the profiles one by one, yet the woman in the Eames Chair remained elusive, as did any other woman who could have fit her profile. The mystery persisted, leaving us with more questions than answers in our quest for clarity about his past and present connections.

'Many of the profiles were private,' Sophia noted, resignedly acknowledging the roadblocks of social media.

'Of course they were,' I replied, my tone carrying a hint of annoyance as if pointing out the obviousness of the situation.

She turned to me with a request. 'Could you follow some of the ones I'd like to know more about?'

'No chance,' I protested, my disbelief evident in the furrow of my brows. 'What are we, sixteen?'

She gave me that exaggerated, desperate look, her face practically begging as her lips mimed a silent 'please'. Unable to disappoint her, I rolled my eyes and handed over my phone.

'Fine, take it. I'll be in the bathroom, coming up with ways for you to pay me back.'

Upon my return, I found that one of the profiles Sophia wanted to investigate had already accepted my request. While it wasn't the lady in the Eames Chair, it was someone equally fashionable. The woman had shoulder-length, wavy blonde hair, though, in some photos, it magically transformed into perfectly straight strands. She seemed to revel in being photographed, showcasing a buoyant smile and rehearsed poses. Scrolling through her extensive profile of over a thousand photos, there was no trace of Giorgio. Instead, there were images of her with other men, and it was obvious she was in her twenties.

'Definitely not her,' I asserted, stealing a French fry from Sophia's plate.

'How do you know?' she inquired, engrossed in the photos and seemingly oblivious to her untouched fries.

'Because she looks like she's twenty in the photo she posted yesterday. If they've been dating for twenty years, he must have asked her out on her first birthday,' I mused.

'Right… you're very observant,' Sophia responded, her eyes still glued to the screen.

'And you're tired. If not, you would have noticed that, too. Let's call it a day on Instagram stalking,' I suggested, gesturing to her to hand my phone back.

Sophia took a deep breath. 'But I hate it when I invest so much time without any results,' she confessed.

'Ask him. You are a woman with a life and a job. You are better than Instagram stalking,' I suggested, finally reclaiming my device.

'You could ask him. He's in Berlin next week. He asked me to meet him there. I wasn't sure if I should go. But with you, it will be fun. Let's have a girl's weekend and meet him for dinner,' she explained, excitement bubbling in her voice.

I opened my calendar on my phone, fully aware that it resembled the vast emptiness of the Sahara. Accustomed to a hectic schedule, the prospect of adding some palms in the desert of my days was irresistible.

Before I could respond, Sophia was making arrangements. 'I'll book at the Adlon. I know you'd like to go back to that one,' she suggested.

'Why not the hotel he's staying at?' I asked, secretly hoping we'd stick to the Adlon.

'No, that would be too much, don't you think?' she turned to me.

'And going through his every connection on Instagram isn't too much?' I teased.

'But he doesn't know that,' she smirked, her mischievous side peeking through.

I loved my friend, but she was acting like a teenager. Then again, it was her relationship, her life, and I couldn't pass up a trip to Berlin.

CHAPTER ELEVEN

'Do not cry because it's over; smile because it happened,' wrote my favourite children's book author, Dr. Seuss, in his book Oh, the Places You'll Go.

The wisdom of Dr. Seuss had always resonated with me, but today, I found myself unable to embrace either the tears or the smiles that usually accompanied my reading of children's stories.

I struggled to recall any fond memories without tainting them with thoughts of him possibly laughing at me, thinking about her while with me, or writing to her during our time together. In hindsight, countless a-ha! and wow! moments revealed themselves, and the pieces of the puzzle finally fell into place. Why did he never invite me to Hamburg? Why avoid FaceTime after a certain hour? Why always visit the hotel reception for extended periods, taking his phone with him during our weekends together? There was nothing positive to salvage from this relationship. The only lesson I might have learned was not to trust men again, and I didn't want to become a cynic. I refused to cry because I did nothing wrong, and there was no one to shed tears for but myself. So, relief seemed the only fitting emotion—an exhale of liberation marking the end of a chapter that warranted nothing more than a sigh. A sigh of relief. Alessia's attempt to infuse hope into the situation was appreciated, but my emotions remained the same. They resembled the grayscale of a nasty storm, just before the rainbow.

'It is a girlfriend. There are no children involved. He can put an end to it with the snap of his fingers,' Alessia insisted, seeking optimism amidst the apparent hopelessness.

As I gazed out of my bedroom window, the raindrops streaking down mirrored the confusion in my mind. Each droplet, like a tiny messenger, seemed to carry a weight similar to the complex emotions I grappled with. Reality loomed over me in shades of grey, uncertain and daunting, much like the stormy clouds hanging low in the sky. My eyes wandered across the apartment; every nook and cranny bore the indelible imprint of his presence. The cosy corners were ruined by the memory of shared moments, and the ambient warmth now felt haunted by his absence. Oh, why did I ever let him into my apartment, my safe space? Even more agonising, why did I let him into my heart? I could still hear Alessia's voice, but I wasn't truly listening. Eventually, she ceased talking, fixing her gaze on me, awaiting a response to a question I couldn't quite pinpoint.

Contemplating the intricacies of the situation, I eventually voiced my thoughts. 'I suppose, theoretically, he could put an end to their relationship, but that doesn't alter the undeniable fact that he deceived me for months. Or, actually, he deceived her. I was the affair in this triangle.' It was a perspective I hadn't really considered before, but it was the reality. Whether that fact made me feel better or worse, I wasn't sure.

As I looked at Alessia, she returned my gaze, her silence speaking volumes. Perhaps she feared saying the wrong thing, something I didn't want to hear. Turning my attention to the window again, the world outside seemed pensive at that moment.

After a drawn-out, grounding breath, I continued. 'But do I really want a relationship with someone who's trying to balance on two chairs, knowing he could topple them both at any time? And I'm not even sure what his intentions are. He could've ended things after meeting me or at least been upfront about his feelings before dropping the L-bomb.'

Alessia, always ready with sage advice, felt compelled to lift my spirits after my emotional confession. 'You're a fabulous chair, darling. You deserve a man who's all-in, someone who knows exactly where he wants to sit—and that's with you.'

Alessia's remark would usually spark laughter from me, but in that moment, it felt like humour had left the building. Our conversation hung heavy in the air, burdened by unanswered questions. The dim white glow of the table lamp seemed to amplify the solemnity of the atmosphere as if searching for colour in a world drained of it. Trust and honesty, once vivid hues, now felt muted by the overly-pigmented brushstroke of deception.

Amidst this emotional storm, the upcoming trip to Berlin with Sophia felt like a ray of light finally breaking through the clouds. The city's lively energy promised a distraction and, if only for a while, a respite from the gravity of recent revelations and the emotions swirling in my heart as a result.

...

Berlin, undoubtedly, has witnessed tragedies far more profound than the one I was going through.

With its mix of history and contemporary charm, the city felt like the ideal setting for renewal. Our journey to Berlin wasn't just about travelling to a familiar destination; it symbolised a potential path to healing and self-discovery, a chance to find comfort amidst the bustling cityscape. Still, it would have been even better if Alessia could join us on that Berlin adventure. It had been too long since the three of us had gone on a girls' trip together. Recent commitments had claimed her time, and her absence was deeply felt.

We could hardly blame her, though. Alessia was diving headfirst into an exciting adventure as she launched her very first beauty clinic. In a shockingly short amount of time—maybe just a few weeks, definitely not more than two months—she'd taken a dream and turned it into a full-blown business.

With six years of dermatology know-how, she had all the skills and a loyal network of patients. However, she was itching to break free from the restrictions of someone else's clinic. The lightbulb moment happened during a casual chat on the ride home after a fancy dinner, where the wine flowed as freely as the conversation.

That night, with her closest friends and biggest fans hanging onto her every word, Alessia spilt about her frustrations with the old-school ways of doing things. In one instance, she had this bold idea to tackle a stubborn psoriasis case in a totally new way, but her boss wasn't having any part of it.

That's when Sophia, in all her wisdom, dropped the mic with a simple question: 'So, why don't you just do it your way?'

Known for her rebellious streak and aversion to following the crowd, Alessia had always danced to the beat of her own drum. But when it came to her professional life, she habitually found herself tangled up in someone else's rules. As a passionate doctor deeply in love with her work, Alessia's biggest gripe came from outside forces hindering her innovative ideas to help her patients.

In her grand vision for her clinic, Alessia set out to shake up dermatological care beyond the usual list of prescriptions. Instead of just slapping on topical treatments, she championed the proactive power of a good diet as the cornerstone of well-being. Her approach wasn't just about fixing skin issues; it was about detoxing, preventing issues before they arose, boosting overall appearance, and promoting self-confidence. Alessia emphasised the importance of a holistic lifestyle that complemented her dermatological expertise, creating a comprehensive strategy for her patients' overall health and beauty.

As Alessia's beauty clinic took shape, it was clear her approach was something special. Beyond doling out dietary tips and supplements, her office offered a whole range of services. From helping you pick the perfect cosmetics for your skin type to promoting hair growth, perfecting posture, and battling stubborn fat and cellulite, this place had it all. And while they skipped the permanent makeup, they weren't shy about offering Botox, fillers, lasers, and more.

Alessia's boldness and drive were on full display as she chased her dream of being her own boss. For her, entrepreneurship wasn't just about making bank; it was about taking risks, making a difference, and going after what you want with all you've got.

As we geared up for our Berlin escapade with Giorgio, it was clear that Alessia couldn't join the party. But she made sure to hand us a fancy invite to her clinic's grand opening. She was pumped about the idea of Giorgio showing up. Sophia was grateful for the invitation, but there was a hint of uncertainty in her response. While he was approachable and friendly, he became reserved when conversations turned deeper. Travelling to Munich to meet her friends seemed like a big ask at that point. She feared he might think she was rushing things, imposing expectations he wasn't ready to meet, and that he might back off. She hated that she once again had expectations from a man.

'It will also be good for the business to have international guests present,' Alessia remarked. 'To build out our network.'

'You are such a good friend, thank you,' Sophia said.

'You are my best friends, but my clinic is my baby,' Alessia responded, her face decorated with a prideful smile.

Sophia gave her an absent smile back. I knew that she still hadn't given up the idea of having a baby. Her 41st birthday was next month, and she said she wasn't feeling like celebrating. I was afraid that the Englishman didn't want to have children. If he did, he probably would have had a few during his twenty-year relationship. Regardless, it was definitely too early for that discussion. They weren't even dating, but they were talking every day over the phone. Some days, for hours–and that wasn't nothing. She grinned from ear to ear every time she spoke about him and blushed when we asked what they were talking about.

'Ah, the usual,' she would say, blushing.

'You're having sex over the phone, aren't you?' Alessia teased her.

'I don't want to talk about it,' Sophia tried to act cool.

'I'm not judging. It is your right,' Alessia said, grinning at me.

I didn't ask any further questions. I knew that if Sophia wanted to tell me, she would. I also knew that she was afraid to admit that she had great expectations and feared that it would be a great disappointment. Again.

CHAPTER TWELVE

I could feel Sophia's genuine excitement about seeing Giorgio again, and I was sincerely happy for her. For me, the prospect of our upcoming weekend in Berlin was a welcomed distraction from the complexities of my own feelings about Daniel and the stinging memories of our past relationship. I viewed the trip as an escape from my thoughts. I hoped to leave my memories of Daniel at the train station in Munich and arrive in Berlin with nothing but the expectation of a fabulous weekend—and a trolley full of even more fabulous outfits, of course.

Daniel's involvement with someone else had severed any remnants of what we once had, leaving me feeling adrift, fragile, and directionless. It was akin to that familiar disappointment when you eagerly bring out your summer clothes, only to be met with an unexpected cold front.

The weather, much like the people we encounter, proves to be unpredictable. You find yourself frustrated with the circumstances, a blend of anger, sadness, and annoyance. The initial enthusiasm to go out fades, and you stay home, allowing the negative emotions to intensify. Then, eventually, the warm summer days arrive. Some are fortunate to have friends to share the sunshine with. In my case, Sophia believed I was doing her a favour by accompanying her to Berlin to meet the Englishman, but little did she know she was the one rescuing me from my own emotional winter.

Thinking of Berlin immediately brings to my mind the iconic Brandenburg Gate. A close second is the delightful breakfast experience at Hotel Adlon. This association is unsurprising, given that my visits to Berlin have coincided with the twice-yearly Fashion Week, centred around the Brandenburg Gate. Nestled next to this historic landmark is Hotel Adlon, and for Sophia and me, one of the many highlights of Fashion Weeks past was undoubtedly our breakfasts there. Amidst the chaos and glamour of the events, we seemed to be the only ones eagerly anticipating the mornings, thanks to that legendary breakfast spread. It felt like a secret indulgence amidst the buzz of Fashion Week, one that only we knew about.

When I roam through a city, my ultimate touristy concoction involves fashion, history, and, of course, fashion history. Berlin Fashion Week, set against the backdrop of its many landmarks, effortlessly showcased this blend of my interests.

The city was like a treasure chest, home to landmarks that each had their own stories to tell. The Reichstag stands proud and iconic, calling out with the promise of panoramic views from its rooftop terrace. Then there's Charlottenburg Palace, dripping with grandeur, royal vibes and stories of regal life. Moving on to the Memorial of the Berlin Wall, the air hangs heavy with the weight of history, a stark reminder of a divided past. A hushed reverence envelops the Holocaust Memorial, its profound stillness cutting through the city's liveliness.

Yet, Berlin's not solely focused on the past. The East Side Gallery bursts with creative urban art splashed across what's left of the Berlin Wall. And then there's the Ku'damm, buzzing with the energy of modern city life.

As I explored these spots on my two trips, I couldn't help but be amazed at how Berlin seamlessly blends its robust history with the modern vibe of today. Each stop felt like flipping through the pages of a story that grabbed you from the first page, with a mix of highs and lows throughout, but always ending on a high note.

Amidst the lively hustle of Berlin, the intersection of fashion and history was always a recurring spectacle. At the recent Berlin Fashion Week, Sophia and I found ourselves immersed in the creative genius of designer William Fan. His collection, housedin the iconic Berlin Television Tower, wove together the contemporary fabric of present-day Berlin with the evocative threads of his Asian ancestry, creating a stunning fusion of two cultures.

What made this event even more special was its venue; it was the first-ever fashion show held in the Berlin Television Tower. To reach the runway, we rode the elevator up to the 'Sphere' restaurant perched 203 meters high in the tower's dome. Its silhouette etched itself into my memory. Every time I see that tower, I can't help but think of the tip of a Christmas tree.

As we settled into our seats, anticipation swirled in the air and was mingling with the panoramic views of the city stretched out beneath. Fan's collection began to unfurl, each piece a harmonious mixture of tradition and modernity. From luxurious fabrics to intricate patterns, his Asian roots were evident, yet he seamlessly infused them with the notoriously edgy vibe of Berlin.

Within the Sphere's retro ambience, models sashayed past tables to the easy beats of classic 80s tunes, all against the backdrop of an awe-inspiring 360-degree view of the city. William Fan's latest collection paid homage to Berlin in the most unexpected ways, like golden TV Tower miniatures embellishing jackets and logo tees boasting prints of the city's iconic landmarks. Of course, everyone was eagerly awaiting the fresh take on his famous fortune cookie bags.

The show wasn't just highlighting women's fashion; Fan seamlessly integrated seemingly masculine pieces that showcased his commitment to diversity and gender-fluid style. While his signature silhouettes remained intricate, there was a noticeable shift towards more figure-hugging designs during the show.

In Berlin, fashion isn't confined by traditional gender norms—it's truly a playground of endless possibilities. Here, you can rock any style, colour, or silhouette you fancy without worrying about fitting into a predetermined box. In plain terms, fashion is just another way to express yourself. And in Berlin, self-expression is king. It's all about embracing the 'anything goes' mantra. From classic French chic to minimalist vibes and from smart casual to boho-chic, gothic, artsy, and beyond, Berliners aren't afraid to mix it up. Clothes aren't just clothes here; they're statements, they're art.

What sets Berlin's fashion apart is the unexpected mix of styles. High fashion meets street style, cosy knits seem natural up against sleek leather, and simple looks perpetually get a pop of colour or a bold print. Speaking of colour, Berliners aren't shy about going bold. Every hue imaginable finds its place in this place.

But what's even more remarkable is the attitude held by everyone here. In Berlin, you wear what you want, and nobody bats an eye. People are too busy chasing their own dreams to worry about what others are wearing. It's a city that celebrates individuality and creativity in all its forms, fashion included. In a place where art saturates every aspect of life, from the streets to galleries, the expectation is nothing short of a creative and daring fashion sense.

The clock had struck midnight as we stepped onto the platform at Berlin's central train station. Sophia dialled Giorgo's number twice, but there was no answer. It was then she revealed a detail she had kept from me: the fact that Giorgo was unaware of our arrival. Initially, Sophia had declined his invitation to meet in Berlin, only to change her mind later without informing him. This trip was meant to be a surprise. Had I known, I would have cautioned against it; surprises and I had a somewhat tumultuous relationship. Nevertheless, she wasn't alone this time, and we weren't stranded at the station; we had hotel reservations and a plan.

As we strolled along the Spree, our trolleys in tow, we took in the city's lively atmosphere. The one-kilometre journey to the hotel offered a chance to catch some fresh air and appreciate the busy streets of the city centre we had just spent the evening looking out upon. It was a Friday night, and the energy was palpable. Our weariness from the travel day lingered, and going out seemed like an implausible proposition... at first.

'Feel like dancing?' Sophia's eyes lit up, excitement practically radiating off her as she posed the question.
'Yes?' I replied, stifling a yawn that betrayed my exhaustion. Even so, the idea of hitting the dance floor stirred something in me—a flicker of intrigue that danced around, despite my weary body.

Berlin's nightlife is legendary, with clubbing considered a serious affair—so much so that there's rumoured to be an unspoken 'clubbing etiquette'. Stories have circulated of folks getting turned away for daring to wear white jeans or the wrong pair of high heels. So, dear reader, if you're planning to hit up a Berlin club: be sure to scout the dress code on the establishment's website—it's the key to a successful entry.

My own experiences in Berlin have mostly revolved around fashion weeks, where post-show club visits were a common occurrence. Those nights were ripe with elegant dresses and sky-high heels. But on this particular outing with Sophia, it wasn't fashion week, nor did we have an invite to an exclusive after-party. It was just a regular Friday night out.

For the occasion, I opted for faux-leather skinny trousers paired with a black crop top and Saint Laurent sneakers—low-key branding because, as Sophia reminded me, 'Logo is a no-go.' Meanwhile, Sophia rocked a pair of dark blue cargo pants, an off-shoulder top in red, and white sneakers, all subtly sporting the Off-White branding, if my memory serves me right. Despite the ultra street-style vibe of her cargo pants, she somehow managed to exude a more French than Berliner aesthetic.

Sophia sighed, 'I can never pull off looking cool. And I've never worn these trousers before.'

I chuckled, 'I believe you. I've never owned a pair of cargo pants myself, although I do think they look pretty cool on others.'

We both threw on denim jackets. Sophia's pick was a short and structured piece, while I opted for my recently acquired oversized jacket from Acne Studios. In Munich, chances to flaunt denim outerwear were few and far between. Yet, there's something about denim that still feels inherently youthful and alluring.

Calvin Klein famously declared, *'Jeans are sex. The tighter they are, the better they sell,'* causing a stir with an iconic ad featuring the 15-year-old Brooke Shields and the bold tagline that read: *'Do you know what comes between me and my Calvins? Nothing.'*

Despite the controversy, the ad catapulted Calvin Klein denim into the spotlight. Over the years, denim, once a humble utility wear, has morphed into a luxury category of its own. It begs the question: why do we willingly splurge on pricey jeans when denim is so readily available? The answer lies in how denim has managed to retain an air of exclusivity while still remaining a wardrobe staple for all.

The shift in perception of jeans as a fashion item, rather than an antifashion item, can be credited to Warren Hirsch. In 1976, Hirsch proposed the idea to Gloria Vanderbilt, a member of one of America's most affluent families, to endorse a line of upscale jeans. He believed there was a market for jeans that sounded elitist. Vanderbilt agreed, and the jeans quite literally flew off the shelves. The versatile nature of jeans, simultaneously gender-neutral and sexy, democratic yet exclusive, timeless yet infused with the illusion of youth, is truly remarkable when you think about it.

Nevertheless, this chapter isn't about denim; instead, it revolves around Berlin, Sophia, and her newfound romantic interest. So far, we haven't had the chance to see the last one sporting jeans. However, our experiences have included glimpses of denim-clad icons like David Beckham, Ryan Reynolds, and James Dean.

Berlin. We went dancing. The next morning, Giorgio called Sophia back. He didn't mention anything about not answering her calls yesterday, which left her feeling a bit frustrated.

'Maybe he was sleeping?' I suggested.

Sophia shook her head. 'He would have said so. He would have said, "Oh, I'm sorry. I just saw your call; I was sleeping…" or something.'

'Something like… "I wasn't expecting you to call because you said you couldn't make it this weekend, and that is precisely why I wasn't checking my phone?!"' I simply stated what was obviously the case. It is much easier to keep an open mind and a level head when you are not emotionally involved.

Sophia nodded, 'Yes, he wasn't expecting me, so he made other plans. I guess there was someone who said yes immediately.'

I tried to reassure her, 'I think you are overthinking it. So, when are you, or we, meeting him?'

'Oh, we're not. I told him that we had plans and that I would call him.'

'No, you didn't. Seriously? We don't have plans. Actually, we do… to meet him,' I slapped my palm to my forehead, silently asking myself why she was being this difficult.

'Sophia, you are my favourite person in the world, but I hate this kind of behaviour. You are not a small girl who is afraid to say how she feels or what she wants. You are a successful and busy woman who took a five-hour train ride to this city to have fun with the guy you like and to find out if there could be something more than that. I'm always here to back you up, but I am not encouraging this. Call or text him now that we will meet him for dinner. Let him pick a place. After dinner, you can have some private time together and talk about yesterday if you want to know more about it.'

Sophia paused for a beat, her expressive eyes widening with surprise as my very direct words sank in. I could practically see the gears turning in her mind, weighing the truth of what I'd just said. The room fell silent as she processed, and I couldn't help but feel a mix of annoyance and concern for my friend.

In that fleeting moment, I caught a glimpse of vulnerability in Sophia's usually confident demeanour. It was like my words had pricked a hole in the protective bubble she'd built around herself. I knew her well enough to recognise that this wasn't the fearless Sophia who tackled challenges head-on.

She excused herself to the bathroom, closing the door behind her. As I gazed out the window, I found myself contemplating the intricacies of friendship and adulthood. My frustration at Sophia's indecision clashed with my genuine desire to see her find the happiness she deserved.

I debated my next move—should I push her to open up more, or give her the space to sort through her feelings? Below the double hung window, the streets of Berlin buzzed with life, blissfully unaware of the emotional storm brewing in our hotel room.

After what felt like an eternity, Sophia emerged from the bathroom, her posture a mix of resolve and uncertainty. Her words cut through the silence, 'We're meeting him at seven at Ishi.'

'Really?' I raised an eyebrow.

Sophia nodded, the faintest hint of excitement in her eyes. 'Yes, I just called him and asked where to meet him for dinner, like you said.'

'No, I meant, really, Ishi? He's Italian. I thought we would be having ravioli for dinner when I said to let him choose. Not Japanese.' I smiled and then thought about the first time I met her ex; it was a sushi kind of dinner, too. She shifted her gaze toward the window behind me. 'Should we go jogging? I will feel less guilty at breakfast if we do.'

Jogging together was a rarity for us, and as we made our way to the lobby, I found myself reflecting on the last time we hit the pavement.

'So, what is Maurice doing today until dinner?' I inquired casually.

Sophia's expression shifted, and she went quiet for a moment.

'Who?' she asked, though it was clear she knew I had mistaken the name.

'Oh, sorry. I meant Giorgio. What is Giorgio doing today?' I mentally berated myself for the slip-up, mixing his name with her ex. 'He has some meetings, I guess,' she replied absentmindedly.

I hoped the slip-up didn't dampen Sophia's excitement about seeing Giorgio later that day. It was clear she was nervous and a bit sceptical. I could imagine the questions lingering in her mind: What had he done the night before? Why didn't he answer his phone? If he was already sleeping, why not mention it when he called in the morning? Cold feet were setting in, but nonetheless, she confidently put on her favourite high heels that evening.

Sophia had owned those sexy Yves Saint Laurents since I first met her, and they still looked as pristine as if she bought them yesterday. Her meticulous care for her shoes made me incredibly proud. A tip I often share with friends: Never wear shoes that look old and worn out; it can ruin the entire look and negatively impact your image. Beyond that, it affects your arches, ankles, posture, and overall health. We wear shoes. And then they wear out.

Sophia was a vision in her black silk knee-length Victoria Beckham dress. The slim fit and sleeveless silhouette with a round neckline transitioned into a voluminous skirt, capturing the ladylike essence of Victoria Beckham's designs. It looked impeccable, but I wasn't sure if it was the right choice for the occasion. For me, I stuck to the same leather pants and sneakers from the previous night, pairing them with a fancier top and a blazer.

'Are you sure you want to wear this dress in a restaurant where we will probably sit on the floor?' I asked Sophia as she examined herself in the mirror.

'What do you mean?' she replied, turning to me.

'Well, you know, when we were at this Ishi restaurant in the past, the whole space had about ten seats on pillows on the floor.'

'We've never been to Ishi, Elena,' she said, raising an eyebrow.

'Of course we have. It was the cute Japanese place with great food and affordable cocktails, remember?' I bit my lip, attempting to remember more details about our previous dining experience. 'Oh, and now I recall that we were even supposed to take off our shoes as we entered. Are you sure you want to leave these sandals unattended? You know that this style is irreplaceable.'

Sophia burst into laughter, her eyes sparkling with amusement.

'I am dead serious,' I said, unwavering in my memory but still giving her a playful look.

'And you are dead wrong. We were at Ichi Restaurant when you protested about taking off your Chanels. We are going to Ishi tonight.'

'What?' I exclaimed. It sounded the same. It had to be the same. But Sophia knew Berlin much better than I did. I had to Google it.

'Yes, this is Ishi, not Ichi. You see?' We scrolled through the photos on Ishi's website.

'Alright then, this is not the place I thought,' I admitted, feeling a bit embarrassed. Sophia's laughter filled the room.

'Of course not. Why did you even think that Giorgio would suggest that place?' Sophia continued to chuckle as I realised my mistake. The confusion over the restaurant names had lightened the mood, and Sophia's infectious laughter put me at ease. I shook my head in mock disbelief.

'Well, it had this cool, authentic vibe, you remember? The food was outstanding, and the whole atmosphere felt fresh. What I loved most was the privacy—it was the kind of place where you could actually have a decent conversation without having to shout over the crowd. I thought Giorgio wanted to take us somewhere offbeat, but it turns out he had more elegant plans in mind,' I explained.

Sophia nodded and looked down at my feet. 'Okay. So, now that's settled, are you ready to part ways with your sneakers for tonight?'

'Absolutely!' I replied with a grin, Slipping out of my sneakers, finally getting into the spirit of the evening.

The prospect of elegant Japanese dining in Berlin, coupled with Sophia's contagious excitement, set the tone for a night filled with delightful surprises. However, as the events actually unfolded, some less delightful ones also emerged.

As Sophia and I made our way towards the address, I couldn't tear my eyes away from her. It was like seeing a whole new side of my friend. She was beaming with a level of excitement I hadn't witnessed since the day she brought home her first Birkin. I chose to stay quiet, not wanting to interrupt the genuine joy that lit up her face—it suited her. Among her captivating features, her shiny blonde hair stood out to me that evening. Cascading gracefully to her shoulders, it glistened with a natural sheen that complemented her radiant presence. What fascinated me was how it moved with her, swaying and dancing as she walked, as if it had a mind of its own.

Stepping into the restaurant, Ishi was clearly a whole different ball game from the casual Ichi I had in mind. I was grateful that we were spared from partaking in the tradition of leaving our shoes at the entrance that night.

Sophia, always the diplomat, warned me against probing too much, fearing it might ruffle Giorgio's feathers. She had a knack for sidestepping anything that could lead to confrontation or awkwardness—it was just her being her usual thoughtful self, perhaps to a fault.

'Oh, come on. He's Italian and lives in the UK. I'm sure he's used to a bit of directness,' I suggested, attempting to ease Sophia's nerves.

'Please, just no questions,' she hushed me as we followed the hostess to our table. We assumed Giorgio hadn't arrived yet, but he slid into view the very next second and promptly pulled out Sophia's chair for her.

'You look lovely,' he complimented her.

'This is my friend Elena,' Sophia introduced me, a touch of nervousness in her voice.

'I know Elena. I gave you a ride in Venice with my taxi, remember? And please, feel free to ask anything you want,' he added with a wink, smiling warmly and pulling me into a friendly embrace. The scent of his cologne triggered memories of that day in Venice.

Of course, I had met him. Sophia was visibly on edge. We quickly realised that as we followed the hostess to our table, we passed by Giorgio, who was engrossed in a conversation with someone at another table. Unbeknownst to us, he caught wind of our presence. Sophia grew even more jittery after Giorgio's playful nod to the fact that he overheard her telling me not to probe. It was yet another side of her I hadn't witnessed before; she genuinely liked the guy. In an attempt to ease her nerves, I placed my hand on her leg, offering silent support.

Feeling famished after our jog, I eagerly reached for the edamame on our table, served with three unusual toppings. As I popped the first pod into my mouth, a burst of flavours hit me — a delightful fusion of nuttiness from the sesame, the zing of scallions, and a hint of saltiness, creating a perfect prelude to the culinary journey that would follow. Soon after, the server presented an assortment of sashimi on an elegant platter. The delicate slices of impeccably fresh fish showcased the chef's precision, each piece showcasing the artistry of Japanese culinary craftsmanship. With a dab of wasabi and a light dip in soy sauce, the sashimi melted on my tongue, leaving behind the essence of the ocean.

The dining adventure continued with Ishi's signature sushi rolls. The Dragon Roll, a work of art, featured avocado slices perfectly draped over a core of shrimp tempura and crabmeat, topped with a drizzle of unagi sauce. Each bite offered a delightful medley of textures — the crunch of tempura, the creamy avocado, and the savoury seafood, all tied together by the sweet notes of the unagi sauce. For the main course, we were presented with what can only be described as a masterpiece: miso-glazed black cod. The dish was truly a culinary marvel, its tender flesh soaking up the sweetness of the glaze, creating a crescendo of flavours that left me craving more. What can I say? Japanese cuisine holds a special place in my heart.

But beyond my love for food, I also have a soft spot for good humour. And let me tell you, the night with Giorgio was a riot. His charm was effortless, his sarcasm cutting, his wit razor-sharp... he kept the entire table entertained. As Giorgio and I traded banter, our laughter filling the air, I couldn't help but notice Sophia's uncharacteristic silence. Her gaze lingered on me, a mix of concern and curiosity in her eyes, perhaps wondering if Giorgio's jokes would rub me the wrong way. To her surprise, and mine as well, I welcomed the laughter on a weekend that initially seemed destined for tears.

Concerned that she might misinterpret the dynamic between myself and Giorgio, I decided to invite her into the sanctuary of the ladies' room—a space where unspoken thoughts often found their voice. As we stepped inside, the distant chatter of the restaurant faded away, leaving us in a cocoon of privacy.

'I don't know,' Sophia admitted, unease evident in her voice. 'I just started to get a bad feeling about him. And he still hasn't mentioned anything about yesterday—no apology for not returning my call earlier, for not joining us, nothing.'

'Don't read too much into it,' I said, hoping to calm her nerves. 'Sometimes our instincts can be misleading.'

'Don't you also have the feeling that he is hiding something?' Sophia questioned, her eyes searching mine in the reflection of the mirror.

'Isn't everyone hiding something?' I retorted, nonchalantly checking my makeup. Sophia shot me a sceptical look. 'You are hiding that you're mad at him because he didn't answer your call yesterday. You are hiding that you really like him. I am hiding my breasts from his friend, who can't stop staring at my décolleté,' I quipped.

Sophia burst into laughter so loudly that I half expected Giorgio and his friend to hear us behind the doors. That friend, by the way, was an unexpected addition to the party. Actually, he appeared to be more of an accidental addition—a last-minute inclusion prompted by Sophia's spontaneous decision to bring me along.

The friend, whose name escaped my memory even toward the end of the night, seemed to embody awkwardness in both appearance and demeanour. Throughout the entire meal, he remained a silent bystander, his presence marked by a rigid posture and a distant stare. Despite my usual proficiency with names, his eluded me, speaking to the utterly unremarkable impression he made.

'He's a nice guy, just a bit slow. You know, the lights are on, but nobody's home,' Giorgio confided to Sophia after the dinner, a lighthearted attempt to offer an explanation for his friend's taciturn nature. The Nobody's Home Guy, as Giorgio humorously dubbed him, had become a mere footnote in the evening's unfolding drama.

To conclude our Japanese culinary voyage, we indulged in a selection of mochi ice cream, each delicate ball in my favourite flavours: coconut, mango, raspberry. As we savoured the sweet finale, an unexpected revelation punctuated the air. In a moment seemingly unrelated to any ongoing conversation, Giorgio's silent companion casually mentioned that he, too, had experienced the institution of marriage. Sophia and I weren't particularly interested in stories about his private life, but the fact that he said 'me, TOO' was crucial in this confession, considering it indirectly revealed something about Giorgio's past relationship status. Something that Giorgio had not yet shared with Sophia.

The innocuous statement lingered in the air, sparking a pregnant pause filled with unspoken inquiries.

Sophia, her curiosity trumping her tact, wasted no time in asking, 'Who else has been married?'

All eyes turned to Giorgio, who, with a subtle nod, confirmed the revelation. The Nobody's Home Guy, in his Nobody's Home fashion, disclosed, 'Well... Giorgo.'

The bombshell revelation cast a shadow over the dinner table, and Sophia's expression combined a blend of surprise, intrigue, and perhaps a hint of rage. With this unexpected twist, our dinner took a sharp turn into complicated territory. We were now knee-deep in unexpected revelations and the messy layers of personal histories.

'I thought you said you weren't married,' I could overhear Sophia saying while Giorgo was closing the door of my taxi.

'I didn't say I wasn't married before.'

'No, I exactly remember that you said that you were together for twenty years and you broke up. Not that you divorced.'

'And that is the truth. I was married before that.' Giorgio's new revelation left Sophia, and me, stunned.

'But you were a child before that,' Sophia's incredulous tone nearly shouted.

'I was 21. Just finished university. She was 24. She got pregnant. We got married. Not because of the baby, though. I knew I wanted to marry her the day I saw her. We just pulled everything together a bit faster when we found out that she was expecting. And then everything fell apart. She was still 24 when they died in the car crash.'

'They?' Sophia's voice wavered, struggling to process the weight of what he was telling her.

'She and our baby in her stomach. She and my daughter,' Giorgo explained, his voice cracking.

'A girl?' Sophia managed to ask.

'The due date was supposed to be yesterday's date, 23 years ago,' Giorgo shared, his gaze fixed on his hands. 'Each year, on that date, I go to bed as early as possible to shorten the day as much as possible. I couldn't get out of bed around that date for years. It was supposed to be the happiest day of my life. I don't have many happy days in my life at all, now.'

'Not the day you met her?' Sophia's voice trembled with empathy, tears welling up in her eyes.

'No. I wish I had never met her. She would have been alive now, probably.'

'You can't know that.' Sophia struggled to hold back her tears, with one escaping down her cheek.

'I am sorry for making you sad. And probably ruining your day,' Giorgo said.

'You didn't ruin my day. But, yes, I am sad,' Sophia replied. 'I can't imagine what you have been through. Not all stories are meant to have happy endings. Yours is endlessly sad. It will always be part of your life, just like sadness is a natural part of life. I am glad that you shared this with me. I feel I know you better now. And I want to be there in your life to see what happens next.'

'I was driving the car,' he said, looking up at her.

Sophia told me later that she felt there was nothing she could or should say. He hadn't mentioned anything about her staying in his life. Maybe, even 23 years later, he wasn't ready to move on—or maybe he wasn't ready to move on with her. And that was okay.

Sophia didn't say a word; she simply wrapped her arms tightly around him, and they stood together in silent comfort for a while. When she told me, I realized there was nothing I could or should say to her either.

...

The next morning, I descended to Bel Etage alone. I am an avid breakfast enthusiast; it's a ritual I never skip. Whether at home or facing an early wake-up call, my go-to is an acai bowl with coconut granola, various seeds, and berries. Egg-based dishes don't quite make it to my list of favourites. However, during my stay at Hotel Adlon, I stumbled upon their Matcha Granola, which surprisingly wasn't a bad addition. What made the breakfast experience even more delightful was the hotel's in-house patisserie. The freshly baked bread, rolls, croissants, and éclairs not only smelled heavenly but tasted as if they were plucked straight from the renowned La Maison d'Isabelle in Paris—a fitting touch for a hotel situated on Pariser Platz in Berlin.

Croissants and éclairs are my ultimate pastry indulgences. I eagerly shared this preference with the hotel's pastry chef while generously loading my plate with an assortment of five distinctly flavoured éclairs. Engaging in conversation with the French chef, I discovered a fascinating tidbit: the croissant derives its name from its crescent moon-like shape. At the same time, éclair literally translates to 'flash of lightning'. Both pastry names draw inspiration from the celestial realm, and indeed, these treats taste heavenly.

I was surprised by the chef's introduction of a passion fruit macaron, a new and irresistible addition to my palette. Featuring pillowy soft shells made with egg whites and almond flour (because that's the only way I prefer my eggs), these macarons were filled with fresh passion fruit curd without any added sugar, topped with marshmallow frosting. Alongside the multitude of macarons in every conceivable flavour, there were drop cookies labelled as macaroons. This marked the moment when I realised these were two distinct cookies. Truly, what a difference an 'o' can make!

Both macarons and macaroons are gluten-free, sharing a crucial ingredient: whipped egg whites. The French macaroon boasts a fluffy texture, while the Italian counterpart is delightfully crunchy. Both varieties have a shared history since their origins can be traced back to mediaeval Italy. In my previous book, I discussed the influential role played by Catherine de Medici in introducing the French to Italian fashion, delicate fabrics, and perfumery, and even being credited with the invention of the first high-heeled shoe—a personal favourite subject of mine. During the Italian Renaissance in the fifteenth century, Catherine de Medici imported not only sophisticated fashion but also refined cuisine to France. She brought along with her cooks, delis, and traditional Italian recipes, including what would later become macarons (known as Italian maccherone). The grandson of Ladurée's founder, Pierre Desfontaines, is credited with the ingenious idea of sandwiching two macaron shells together and filling them with ganache, thus inventing the sophisticated and franchised macaron, much like the one on my gold-rimmed breakfast plate.

Sipping on my second glass of champagne, I received a call from Sophia, who informed me not to wait for her for breakfast. She sounded perfectly okay. I hoped she didn't catch the background noise, deducing that I had no plans to wait for her after all. Without further elaboration, she left me to assume I wouldn't see her until our scheduled check-out time. Fortunately, we had arranged for a late check-out.

I found myself staring at the fountain in the middle of the limestone lobby. The elephant fountain, made of marble and onyx, looked posh against the luxurious backdrop of the hotel.
A voice from behind broke my contemplation. 'It was a gift to Lorenz Adlon from the Maharaja of Patiala.' It was the patissier I had spoken to just a few minutes earlier.

'Who is that?' I inquired, still captivated by the fountain.

'One of the famous guests who stayed at this hotel. Quite extravagant. He was the first Indian citizen to own an aircraft. In 1910, I believe.'

'Hmm,' I mused, 'I was just thinking it looked quite unusual for Berlin. Definitely an Asian design style, now that I've heard the story. I thought that the entire hotel was destroyed during the Second World War. There is not even a scratch on the fountain.' Afterwards, I discovered that the elephant fountain had a Japanese theme.

'Actually, it is an exact replica of the original historic piece. The original one was in the garden and was destroyed at the end of the war, along with much of the hotel. Having avoided the bombs that levelled the city, the hotel nearly survived the war without any major damage. However, on May 2, 1945, a fire started in the hotel's wine cellar, leaving the building in ruins. Legend has it that the fire was started by drunken Red Army soldiers.'

I hushed him abruptly upon hearing the mention of the 'drunken Red Army'. My ears had caught snippets of Russian conversation from the guests at the nearest table. Unfazed, the patissier placed a plate with croissants and strawberries beside my empty glass.

'More champagne?' he inquired, presenting the offer with a warm smile.

'No, thank you. And no more croissants, either,' I declined politely.

'You have to try this one. It's extra crunchy and has no filling—just almonds, coconut flour, and coconut butter. I'm serving it with fresh strawberries.' Sold. There's something undeniably sexy about men who are passionate about food. Chefs, in particular, have a certain something.

'Wow. No eggs?' I was relieved to steer the conversation from war to food.

'I don't like eggs,' he stated matter-of-factly, taking a seat next to me at the small round table. I felt a twinge of guilt for not offering first, as I hadn't expected him to join me during working hours.

'OMG, me either. I thought I was the only one in the world that didn't like eggs. But you make pastries. That's not easy without eggs.'

'There are so many alternatives. I still use eggs. But I also like to experiment, like you. I noticed you testing new flavours and savouring every bite,' he observed, his eyes gleaming with appreciation. 'It's a rare sight. Most people merely pile their plates high, mindlessly consuming without truly relishing what they're eating. There's a lack of joy, no spark of excitement for the unknown. It shouldn't just be about eating; it should be an experience of joy, of sparkles. And, I must say, I witnessed that in you.'

As he spoke, I looked into his playful eyes, and his words carried a palpable passion for his craft. His German sounded joyful with that sweet French touch. While he wasn't particularly good-looking, he exuded an amazing energy that drew me in.

'What is your favourite food?' he asked me suddenly.

'Aside from your croissants, éclairs, and the occasional macaron, I have a taste for savoury delights. Gnocchi in a zesty lemon sauce, spaghetti vongole or with prawns, pizza tartufo, or a platter of sushi. And, of course, I'm mad about fruits. And french fries. Oh, and sushi. Did I say that already?'

'Can I take you out for lunch? I know a place perfectly tailored to your taste,' he proposed, leaning in with an air of anticipation.

'Thank you, but I can't make it for lunch. We're leaving today,' I regretfully declined.

'We?' he inquired.

'Me and my friend,' I clarified.

'I didn't see your friend,' he noted.

'We were together yesterday for breakfast. She had some early appointments today. I didn't see you yesterday,' I mentioned.

'I'm not here often. I am usually at the bakery. I also frequent Munich. I hope you'll give me the chance to see you there,' he expressed with a hopeful smile.

I realised then that I hadn't actually mentioned where I lived. Strange, I thought. But I simply replied, 'Of course.'

'Elena, excuse me, please,' he slowly stood up and floated back to the kitchen, leaving me intrigued by his charming demeanour. And by the fact that he accurately guessed that I live in Munich.

I gazed down at the fountain again. In my mind's eye, I envisioned Marlene Dietrich gracefully occupying the gold-coloured velvet armchair upholstered with embroidered fabrics from Rubelli Venice. The staircase gave off an aura of old-world glamour, its steps bathed in the warm glow of a three-and-a-half-metre-high chandelier boasting 390 glass prisms made of the finest Murano glass by the traditional Venetian manufacturer, Venini. The elegant lobby, hiding under the illuminating domed ceiling, served as a timeless gathering spot for Berlin's elite. Although the large decorative dome ceiling was not crafted in Venice but in Bavaria, Germany, its cobalt blue-flashed glass with silver-yellow paintings paired with sandblasted glass infused a truly Venetian flair. This, coupled with the painted starry sky, bestowed a voluminous sense of space and added a touch of romance to the entire ambience.

In the midst of the late 19th-century charm, European hotels went through a transformation, becoming more than just places to stay—they turned into extravagant social hubs. Taking cues from luxurious American spots like the Waldorf Astoria, new hotels popped up all over the continent, decked out with fancy ballrooms, grand dining halls, classy arcades, cosy smoking lounges, elegant libraries, and trendy coffee shops. Places like the Hotel Imperial in Vienna (1873), the Hôtel Ritz Paris (1898), and the London Ritz (1906) set the bar for luxury, sparking a craze for sophistication in Berlin's Wilhelmine elite circles, the beating heart of the German Empire.

Lorenz Adlon, a well-to-do enthusiast of fine wine and food, orchestrated a grand venture by acquiring two prime properties in the famous district. A maestro of coffeehouses in Berlin at the time, Adlon set out to create a hotel that would rival the glamour of Paris, London, and other European capital cities. With some convincing, he managed to sway Kaiser Wilhelm II, arguing the necessity of a luxurious retreat for Berlin's socialites. This led to Adlon acquiring the historic Palais Redern, a stunning neo-Renaissance masterpiece designed by Karl Friedrich Schinkel in 1830. Thanks to the Kaiser's backing, Adlon's vision came to life, albeit at the expense of the historic structure.

Conceived by the visionary minds of Carl Gause and Robert Leibnitz, the hotel emerged as a symbol of modernity in Germany, offering amenities like hot and cold running water, an on-site laundry, and its own power plant for electricity. Despite its unassuming exterior, the hotel was chic, with a grand lobby upheld by towering marble columns, a top-notch restaurant, a trendy café, a cosy palm court, and a ladies' lounge. It also housed a library filled with literary treasures, a music room echoing with classical melodies, a sleek smoking room, a high-end barber shop, a luxury cigar shop, and a plethora of grand ballrooms, each oozing a different flavour of opulence and style. During this time period, it was more than a hotel. It was the beating heart of a fashion-forward society.

On the illustrious evening of October 23, 1907, the grand doors of the Adlon swung open. The Kaiser, accompanied by his wife and a crowd of dignitaries, graced the occasion with their presence. In an instant, the Adlon became the undisputed social hub of Berlin. Celebrities flocked to its doors, and the echoes of that magnificent night reverberated for years to come, forever ingrained in Berlin's social history.

The Adlon is a place uniquely steeped in history, unlike any other hotel in Berlin. It witnessed the infamous moment when Michael Jackson dangled his baby from one of its balcony windows. Sarah Jessica Parker, Penelope Cruz, and Queen Elizabeth have all stayed here, though not together. The hotel hosted illustrious guests like Nikolai Romanov, Thomas Edison, Henry Ford, and Rockefeller throughout its existence. It became the iconic address for celebrities and politicians, with luminaries such as Charlie Chaplin and Franklin Roosevelt during the glamorous era of the Golden Twenties.

A century later, it was me who was occupying the petite round table, my champagne glass now empty, and a red-stained plate bearing the remnants of strawberries and the delightful croissant crumbs. Despite the well-dressed guests around, the scene before me diverged from the vivid images etched in my mind. Yet, one element remained untouched: The bellhops, resplendent in their historical uniforms, retained an air of authenticity. Their attire, featuring the brimless blue cap modelled after a 19th-century military drummer boy's hat, complete with a chinstrap, added a distinctive touch rarely seen in my hotel experiences. As Sophia and I stepped into the grandeur of the hotel lobby two days ago, a stern-looking concierge offered the first welcome on our third trip to Berlin.

The pastry chef remained a mystery for the rest of our time in the city. Although he suggested meeting up in Munich, he never asked for my contact info. Maybe he was just being nice, or maybe he found someone else to grab lunch with that day and forgot about our exchange altogether. I gave him some insider tips on Munich's best spots for croissants, but the idea of him waiting for me there felt a bit off. I hoped he wouldn't show up; that would be pushing it into creepy territory. The fact that he already knew that I lived in Munich before I even mentioned it added an unsettling vibe.

To my surprise, we did run into each other in Munich later on. Seeing him at the store sparked a weird tension. My initial instinct was to bolt, thinking he might be some sort of stalker. But it turned out he wasn't—well, maybe just a tiny bit. What he didn't mention in Berlin, or maybe chose not to, was that he had seen photos of me in a magazine article about our trip to Venice with Sophia. In the article, he found out about my connection to the store and recognised my face from our encounter at the hotel, where I gobbled down his croissants. He admitted he thought about cracking a joke about whether the fancy dresses in the photos would still fit, but hesitated, unsure of my reaction.

'Of course, they still fit. They are stretchy,' I responded with a wink. It dawned on me that I was becoming somewhat well-known. Was it a comforting feeling? I couldn't quite decide.

CHAPTER THIRTEEN

'He spoke about you. Not directly, though. I saw this luxurious silk robe hanging in the bathroom.'

I shook my head, denying any connection to a silk robe at his place. Nothing of mine had ever found its way into his apartment.

Before I could respond, Veronica continued, 'When I inquired about its owner, he hesitated, much like you are now. It was as if he was drawing up a story in his mind. Eventually, he claimed to have bought the robe for a girl he used to see. According to him, she once mentioned lounging around in silk and sipping rosé on his library sofa while he played the piano. The girl never returned to live out that fantasy, so he offered me the robe. I sensed a sadness in his eyes, and I wanted to dig deeper, but he remained silent.' She sighed. 'That night, as we passed by the store, he asked if I had been there. When I asked why, he simply mentioned liking the shoes. That same sad, distant look returned. I knew he had no knowledge of women's footwear. I was intrigued, so I visited the store the next day, uncertain of what I was actually looking for until you came over and asked if I'd like a glass of rosé. It was the same rosé that filled half his fridge. I still wasn't convinced it was you, as any girl at the boutique could have fit the description. So, I engaged in small talk to unravel the mystery.'

'And here I thought you were just being polite and friendly,' I eyed her. 'The only thing of interest to me is that we won you over as a customer,' I admitted, revealing a portion of the truth. 'And you are one of my favourite customers,' I added, and I really meant it. In a way. The endearing nicknames no longer felt appropriate, perhaps a silent acknowledgement of the changing dynamics between us. If Javier were to ask, I'd explain that she's the girlfriend of a guy I was seeing some time ago, but we were never in an actual relationship. Now, she's with him, and she even ended up with my silk robe. I'm sure he would understand why I can no longer refer to Veronica by the cute Tinkerbell nickname he came up with.

'It was on Friday at the Opera when I recognised the look in his eyes. It was you. You fled from us as if pursued by furies,' she declared, a hint of pride resonating in her voice as if she had unravelled a mystery. However, my feelings could not have been more opposite from hers that evening.

'Oh, right. No, I didn't run. Well, I did, actually, but it was because I wasn't feeling well,' I explained, offering a plausible excuse, one that I hoped didn't come off as made up. Truth be told, it was the honest reason behind my actions.

'He, too, wasn't feeling well after that. I suggested we leave. He didn't oppose it. I suggested splitting up. He didn't oppose that, either.' She said, looking so intensely into my eyes that I had to look down to evade her piercing gaze.

'I'm sorry,' I said genuinely, a touch of regret seeping into my voice. The shared complexity of emotions lingered in the air, neither one of us knowing quite how to proceed.

'You shouldn't be. He's not the easiest person to be around, but his heart is in the right place. And by that, I mean I think his heart is firmly planted in the position of missing you,' her eyes darted around the room, and suddenly my breath quickened.

'You are a lucky girl.' She continued. 'Now, am I getting a discount on these or what?' Veronica faked a smile, her fingers tracing the sleek curves of a black two-striped sandal from the box on the floor.

I smiled, too, and at that moment, it felt awkward and forced, albeit professional. Even though the previous conversation was of a personal nature, I reminded myself that I was at work.

'37.5?'

'Actually, maybe next time,' she said, giving me the shoe back. I noticed her eyes teared up before she turned toward the door.

'Was that Tinker Bell?' Javier took the sandal from my hands a few moments after she walked through the entryway.

'Yes. No. Well, I don't really know. She got my silk robe.'

Javier looked at me, then at the door, then at me again, with a questioning glance.

As the boutique door chimed softly, I wondered if there would even be a next time. I pondered whether the fabric of our stories would continue to intertwine, or slowly unravel instead.

...

I often found myself contemplating the idea of reaching out to The Surgeon. Over a month had passed since Veronica's visit to the store when Sophia arrived to pick me up for dinner.

'Do you know that he's in the car right in front of the store?' Sophia's gaze bore into me, her brow raised.

'Wait, what?' I blinked, trying to process her words. 'You mean, like, right now? In the car? Outside the store?' The situation was unfolding like a scene from a melodramatic rom-com, and I couldn't decide whether to laugh or panic.

'Didn't you know? Did you forget if you asked him to wait here for you?' Sophia asked.

'No, of course not. I'm having dinner with you.' I responded, attempting to conceal my nervousness and infuse some assurance of our plans into my voice.

'Well, he's here. Parked right on the sidewalk in front of the entrance.' Sophia's gesture toward the glass door was like a cue in a suspenseful movie, her expression a blend of curiosity and concern.

My heart skipped a beat as I followed her gaze, spotting the familiar make of his vehicle parked just outside. A surge of emotions rushed through me, a cocktail of surprise and, apprehension and temptation. This unexpected run-in with The Surgeon reignited a whirlwind of feelings I thought I had left behind, and it felt like stumbling upon a chapter of my past I hadn't intended to re-read that soon. The air in the store once again crackled with the weight of unspoken histories and unresolved emotions. As I stepped closer to the entrance, I braced myself for the uncertain implications of this reunion.

...

The long-awaited day was finally on the horizon, marking the realisation of Alessia's dreams as her clinic transformed from a vision to a tangible reality.

Amidst the flurry of preparations, an undercurrent of excitement bubbled beneath the surface. In response to Alessia's invitation, Giorgio was en route to Munich. The connection forged during their previous encounter with Sophia in Berlin lingered, their phone conversations hinting there were depths yet to be explored. Meanwhile, Sophia diligently monitored Giorgio's social media presence, though the elusive 'ex-girlfriend file' yielded no significant updates.

Anticipation soared with the arrival of Giorgio's brother, a momentous occasion as Sophia prepared to meet a member of his family. It was a significant step in their relationship. As we mulled over the prospect of introducing Giorgio's brother to Alessia, I couldn't shake a twinge of apprehension. Would

Alessia appreciate being set up on a potential date, especially on the eve of her clinic's grand opening?

Expressing my concerns to Sophia, I reminded her of Alessia's reluctance towards matchmaking and her limited time to chat with suitors that evening. Despite my reservations, Sophia assured me that Alessia had consented, reasoning that, at the very least, Giorgio's brother could end up becoming a patient at the clinic.

'Well, of course, he will,' I replied optimistically. 'I'm sure he'll be impressed by Alessia and the clinic.' Curiosity then led me to inquire about the brother's relationship status.

Sophia revealed that he was divorced, much like Giorgio. I reminded her, 'Divorced isn't the same as a widower. One is still paying with his wallet, the other with his heart. Mostly, both are emptied.'

...

Livia was also arriving from Stockholm for the grand opening and staying at my place. I found myself in significantly better spirits and more mentally prepared to discuss the less-than-ideal conclusion with Daniel should Livia broach the topic. But why would she? And why would I still dwell on him? I hadn't heard from him since the night we met at the bar at The Charles.

My colleagues from the store, Isabella and Giesele, were also coming to support Alessia. Javier had just returned from visiting his family in Madrid over the weekend. He was bringing Sebastian. Lisa, the dog, was staying home that night. While Javier expressed enthusiasm, there was an undercurrent of restlessness about how his family would react to his new partnership.

Sophia invited Maurice. Alessia, while handling the invitations, happened to run into Martha at the boutique that day. Maurice promptly RSVP'd, confirming their attendance and signalling a positive development in their mother-son relationship.

CHAPTER FOURTEEN

Veronica was spot-on about one thing, beyond her impeccable taste in shoes. The Surgeon was undeniably not the easiest person to decipher. His demeanour often seemed guarded, distant, and difficult to read. I could imagine that those who didn't know him might see him as unfriendly and arrogant, and he appeared unconcerned with others' opinions. I couldn't recall a single instance where he spoke about anyone else. Our conversations spanned across various topics—biology, history, food, music, art, and even fashion—but never touched upon his personal life, relationships, or acquaintances. Strangely, this omission never bothered me; our discussions were so intellectually stimulating that I didn't notice the absence of anything more intimate.

His speech was eloquent but peppered with indifference, never rising in pitch or expressing excitement or passion, even when discussing a subject I knew he cared deeply about. The thought of him losing his temper or raising his voice was inconceivable; he maintained a perpetually calm composure. Similarly, he seemed completely void of the ability to show any sort of passion or abandon.

He always kept his shirt on, literally and figuratively, presenting a consistent image to the world around him. A crisp, well-ironed shirt was his trademark. I marvelled at the flawless state of his clothing, and couldn't help but wonder about the unseen hand behind this perfection. I contemplated the possibility of seeking out his cleaner to gain insights into their remarkable ironing skills, half-jokingly considering the idea of entrusting them with some of my own dresses.

When he did speak, which was a somewhat rare occurrence, it felt akin to immersing oneself in the lyrical verses of Goethe. That quality was something I cherished about him; it added an extra something, a refinement beyond what his impeccable shirts conveyed. When I spoke, he listened attentively, never interrupting. Sometimes, I found myself wondering whether his silence was born out of genuine interest or sheer boredom, rendering him momentarily speechless.

Despite his lack of interest in fashion, he was consistently well-dressed. His colour palette, much like his personality, consisted of dark blue, grey, black, and white. These shades reflected his reserved, stoic, and understated nature, and intentionally or not—it created a sense of mystery and sophistication. Dark blue conveyed his depth and calm demeanour, while grey and black highlighted his seriousness and focus. The crisp white added a touch of purity and precision, mirroring his meticulous attention to detail as a surgeon.

He always maintained a confident posture. This unspoken language of self-assuredness further accentuated his appeal. Conscious of his physical aesthetics, he dedicated time to self-care, embracing a routine that included morning jogs and evening exercises. His dietary habits were mindful, and he approached alcohol with restraint—not to flaunt, but for the intrinsic satisfaction of personal well-being.

I had assumed that his sense of self-contentment was like a shield against external opinions. While some might view his choices as a form of exhibitionism, he remained unfazed, living life on his terms and his terms only. This self-centric existence, though it seemed solitary, oddly suited him, much like the many tailor-made shirts he owned. Authenticity was his hallmark; he never pretended to be anything he wasn't, making him inherently attractive. Intelligence was his silent companion, seamlessly integrated into his being without any need for show. I liked that.

In quiet moments, I often found myself wondering about his professional persona. Did his calm demeanour persist in the operating room, or did the intensity of surgery reveal a different side of him? Was he composed, offering solace to his patients even in the face of medical challenges? I wondered if he ever grappled with the weight of loss, expressing frustration or grief in the privacy of his professional space. I certainly never bore witness to vulnerability of that nature when I was close to him. Did the sterile, clinical environment allow his emotions to be laid bare—moments of exasperation, silent tears, or the echo of a heart heavy with the responsibility of another's life?

His medical talent was undeniable, a comfort to countless patients who found healing in his capable hands. Yet, for me, his unwavering confidence didn't translate to emotional security. I had always yearned for the reassurance of his words, the simple affirmation that I could trust him completely, that he'd be there when I needed him most. I was afraid to show vulnerability in front of him, fearing it might overwhelm him and that he wouldn't have the patience for more drama outside his profession. I grappled with the silent plea for acknowledgement, a declaration that I mattered to him beyond the surface.

On the evening Sophia arrived to take me for dinner, the unexpected sight of his car parked conspicuously in front of the shoe store caught me off guard. I was given no prior notice of his visit, and it was evident that he intended for me to notice. His imposing G Class seemed to almost obstruct the entrance, making certain I couldn't overlook his presence.

Sophia sensed the tension. 'Should I go and tell him that you don't want to see him?' I knew that such a juvenile tactic wasn't her style, and she knew I wouldn't go for it.

'I'll go,' I replied, attempting to maintain an air of nonchalance. But Sophia, a friend of over a decade, saw through the façade. 'How do I look?' I asked.

'Like a crazy woman. But let me help you with your hair.' With Sophia's deft touch on my hair and a quick application of the 4-7-8 breathing technique to quell my rising anxiety, I made my way to the gargantuan black truck outside. Javier sprung to action, assisting my customer and offering to find the perfect size for a pair of black stilettos, allowing me to navigate the situation at hand. The unspoken plan was clear: let him take the lead in the conversation.

'Hey,' I greeted him through the open window on the passenger side, offering a friendly wave.

'Hey,' he replied, stepping out of the car and making his way towards my side. 'Would you like to come in?' His voice betrayed a hint of nerves, a side of him I had never experienced before.

'Should I come in?' I queried, feigning uncertainty and trying my best to appear disinterested. You know that game.

'I would appreciate a moment of your time for a conversation.' He held the car door open, a gesture that conveyed an unexpected blend of vulnerability and sincerity.

I entered the car, and he drove to the parking lot opposite the store. Leaning back in his seat and avoiding direct eye contact, he broke the silence with, 'The performance was truly splendid.'

I looked at him, puzzled. What could he possibly be referring to? I wondered.

'The other day, at the Opera,' he specified.

'Oh. I thought you didn't see it,' I replied quickly.

'How do you know that?' he inquired, turning to me.

Veronica mentioned it during her visit to the boutique. I didn't explicitly confirm it, choosing instead to reply with a simple, 'I didn't see you afterwards.'

'Yes, I actually didn't stay. But... I'm sure it was a magnificent performance. I'm well-acquainted with the piece, and I recognised most of the actors,' he explained nervously.

At that moment, the Opera piece and the acting skills of his acquaintances were the furthest things from my mind. He fell into a contemplative silence again, engrossed in scrolling through his phone. I couldn't help but wonder what was on his screen—was he bored, texting someone, or searching for a forgotten speech he wanted to present to me? As the minutes stretched, I contemplated leaving, debating whether to engage in this extravagant charade. Yet, I hesitated, unwilling to match his apparent childishness.

Eventually, he turned his phone toward me, revealing a photo of me. I was dressed in a striking red dress, seated on the plush grey velvet sofa in his library. The image had been taken about a week before my journey to Copenhagen.

'No, I haven't framed this photograph or tucked it away in a drawer, but nearly every day, I find myself looking at it. A question keeps nagging at me. Even in this moment of your absolute beauty, there's a hint of sadness. Did I ever make you laugh?'

I smiled.

'Okay, there it is,' he said, a slow smile spreading across his face. His gaze drifted to mine, then locked on with an intensity that sent a jolt through me. Deep blue pools, like a hidden cove promising untold treasures, held me captive. A beat of silence stretched. So thick I could cut it with a knife. Then, ever so gently, his hand reached out. It brushed my cheek, a whisper-light caress that sent shivers erupting across my skin. His fingers skimmed my lips, sending a spark dancing down my neck. I couldn't tear my eyes away, my body attuned to his every movement as if in a silent, sensual dance.

'Do you wish to join me for dinner? Anywhere you want,' he offered, to my immense surprise, suggesting a departure from our old routine of dining strictly at his place.

'I'm sorry, I can't. I promised Sophia we would go out together, and she's already waiting for me inside,' I snuck a peek over toward the store to see if Sophia was still around. I felt a rush of relief that I resisted the immediate temptation to say yes to his first attempt.

'Tomorrow, then?' he persisted. I was so glad he did.

'Tomorrow, Alessia is having the grand opening of her beauty clinic,' I shared with pride.

'Your friend Alessia, the dermatologist?' he inquired.

I nodded.

'That is monumental! Please convey my heartfelt congratulations to her,' he exclaimed with such enthusiasm that it caught me off guard.

I was pleasantly surprised that he remembered Alessia's name and occupation, challenging my assumption that he didn't pay attention to my discussions about my friends.

'You should come,' I impulsively added, immediately grappling with regret. While the desire to see him lingered in my heart, I realised tomorrow was Alessia's moment, not ours. Moreover, I knew Alessia harboured reservations about him. How could I retract my invitation? His reaction suggested he hadn't anticipated the invite either.

'I wanted to see you, just the two of us. I mean, there can be people around, in a restaurant, but you know… I'd be glad to meet your friends some other time,' he said, catching me by surprise once again. I was relieved he declined the invitation before I had to rescind it. I had never seen him so nervous before. I nodded, harbouring a secret hope that his inclination for 'just the two of us' but 'in a public place' wouldn't change before our date in two days. The prospect of seeing him outside the confines of his apartment excited me. As I reached for the door handle, he gently grasped my other hand. When I turned to face him, he murmured, 'Sunday at six. I'll pick you up.'

A mixture of anticipation and uncertainty filled the air. It was a significant step for him, and I couldn't predict whether it would lead to progress for us after all this time. I was left with no choice but to wait for the answer over the next two days.

Returning to the store and Sophia's eager curiosity, she prodded, 'What did you talk about?'

'Nothing,' I replied hesitantly. 'Nothing at all.'

'Why aren't you telling me?' Her irritation was palpable.

'I'm telling you the truth. I also expected that we would talk. No, actually, I'm not sure what I expected. I know him, and I know that he doesn't really talk.' I explained.

'So you just sat in his car and listened to his music?' Sophia inquired ironically.

'He asked me out for dinner,' I shared, attempting to downplay my excitement.

'Are you going?' I could sense she already knew the answer.

'Yes, on Sunday. He asked me about tonight, but I said I already made plans with you,' I explained proudly.

'I'm impressed. And so thankful. I wanted to order the sharing menu. You know I cannot order the sharing menu alone.'

'Why not? They can pack the rest for you to take home,' I suggested.

'That is so sad.'

The thought of ordering the sharing menu by herself might be sad for Sophia, but at that moment, I felt so happy. The prospect of Sunday. A first real date. This one felt special. But before that, I shared a menu with Sophia, and the next day, we celebrated Alessia's success.

...

The night of the grand opening arrived, and the atmosphere was electric. The venue was filled with models, celebrities, and, of course, us. Alessia spared no effort to make it a spectacular event. The motto for the evening was 'Beyond Beauty', and the dress code dictated a sea of white attire. Alessia aimed to channel the essence of a white party, inspired by its roots as fundraisers for HIV/AIDS-related charities. White parties symbolised a safe haven where individuals could come together, embrace their true selves, aspire to transform, and collectively make a positive impact.

    The theme beautifully echoed my friend's vision for her latest venture. For Alessia, that night held the profound purpose of reshaping people's perspectives on dermatology and, more broadly, on health itself. It went beyond the surface level of lotions and creams. Cellulite wasn't just a matter of how our legs looked; skin wasn't merely a canvas for makeup or tattoos. Alessia's message cut through the noise, reminding us that every decision we make about what goes into our bodies, the clothes we wear, the cosmetics we use, and even how we soak up the sun leaves a mark on our skin. Whether it's immediately noticeable or gradually appears over time, our daily habits, emotional reactions, responses to stress, and even our moments of relaxation on a sunny beach - all contribute to the story our skin tells.

    Amidst the constant flurry of activity surrounding us and the intricate processes within our bodies, the skin serves as a boundary delineating our inner selves from the external environment. While we might not have control over everything, we do possess the power to change aspects within our reach. Alessia recognised the challenges many face when attempting to navigate the complex world of personal well-being. Often, we find ourselves unsure of where to start or what choices would truly benefit our unique bodies, given our inherent differences.

Alessia envisioned her clinic as a haven where individuals could seek guidance when feeling unwell. It was a place where a patient didn't necessarily need to pinpoint the source of their discomfort to enjoy adequate care. After all, more often than not, we find ourselves in a state of uncertainty when it comes to our well-being. We may sense that something is amiss without a clear understanding of its origin. In such instances, the tendency is to adopt a wait-and-see approach, hoping for improvement. Sometimes, this proves effective; more often, the issue persists, prompting us to conceal it beneath a layer of makeup.

Alessia acknowledged the cyclical interplay between various internal conditions and their outward manifestation on the skin. She imparted to me a wealth of knowledge about how various chronic illnesses can manifest in the skin. Conditions like psoriasis and eczema, for instance, can be exacerbated by stress, a perfect example of the interconnectedness between our mental and emotional well-being and our skin's health.

Alessia emphasised that yellowish or orangish-looking skin may indicate kidney or liver disease, while grey, sallow skin can be associated with specific chronic conditions. Additionally, brown or tan spots on the shins may signal poor blood circulation, potentially progressing to ulcers if left unaddressed. Hormonal imbalances and nutritional deficiencies can also trigger various acne problems, reinforcing the importance of holistic self-care.

In Alessia's comprehensive approach at the clinic, the seven pillars of self-care—mental, emotional, physical, environmental, spiritual, recreational, and social—were beautifully integrated. The clinic aimed to provide not only medical treatments but also counselling, diagnostics, information, a diverse range of sports activities, massages, and various treatments. Spiritual sessions and community involvement were integral aspects of Alessia's vision. The clinic sought to foster a community where individuals could share a common motivation and vision for self-improvement. It was a place where members supported each other on their respective journeys toward a better self.

The ethereal glow of the reception hall was amplified by minimalist white outfits scattered throughout, emphasising the importance of aesthetics. In our lives. In her clinic. The airy atmosphere was created by the soft glow of string lights that intertwined with cascading white flowers. The subtle fragrance of jasmine and lilies wafted through the air, creating an olfactory symphony that complemented the visual perfection she had so intentionally designed.

As the night unfolded, the reception revealed its culinary delights. Alessia's choice of creamy fettuccine with lobster and white asparagus was divine and delicious. The drinks, too, were a work of art. The mixologist whipped up a signature cocktail simply named 'Bianco', a concoction of elderflower liqueur, lychee, and a splash of champagne. It was served in crystal-clear glasses. So elegant. So Alessia.

After the main course, I followed Sophia and her plate of tempting coconut and white chocolate mochis. I let her guide me through the design choices that made this evening and the grand opening possible. Each piece of furniture they'd selected felt intuitively chosen, playing a harmonious role in the overall aesthetics of the beauty clinic. Alessia's visionary attitude, perfectly complemented by Sophia's impeccable taste, had transformed the space into a luxurious sanctuary. I ran my hand along the smooth surface of a sleek marble side table—everything felt thoughtfully placed, fruition of their combined talents. There was truly nothing I would change.

There were plush armchairs upholstered in calming shades of sage green and sky blue. Fresh lilies and orchids in chic vases on the marble tables added a touch of nature, and the modern paintings in neutral tones keep things serene. It was all about getting you in the right mindset to feel your best.

'Do you think she'd let us move in here? Even if just on the weekends. That Seletti sofa is like a dream. And that kitchen? It's everything.'

Sophia knew I wasn't joking. 'Well, she has big plans for the kitchen. Healthy cooking workshops and stuff.'

'I think if we ever want to see our friend again, we'll have to come here on the weekends and take part in those healthy cooking workshops,' I said.

Sophia mused, 'I don't think she would attend the classes. She has someone for that, a cook from Berlin. I suppose he is here too.' Sophia scanned the crowd, divided between the food, the bar, and the DJ booth, searching for any familiar faces.

'Yes, we should talk to the guests, like she warned us— not to each other. Let's do some organic marketing,' I proposed, adjusting and ensuring my white blazer looked impeccable before starting our campaign.

Sophia's eyes lit up. 'Can you believe that over 50 people have already signed up for an appointment after her speech?'

'Well, we can't take credit for those,' I said, acknowledging the overwhelming success of Alessia's grand opening in this luminous sea of white.

Alessia deserved all the credit in the world. When she took the stage to give her speech, she radiated power, beauty, and composure:

'Imagine a world where your deepest desires bloom within reach. We all share that yearning for joy, for ease, for the beauty that surrounds us. We yearn for love's warmth, the depth of meaningful connections, and the confidence that shines when we feel truly comfortable in our own skin. My hope for you today, esteemed guests, is to ignite that spark within. Discover a love for your body, a celebration of the unique light you bring to this world. Let inspiration, not comparison, guide your interactions.

Your journey is one of continuous growth, uplifting others as you better yourself. Embrace the healthy balance of body and mind, for the challenges we face, are the very things that sculpt us into our most authentic selves.

Today is the start of a transformation. This clinic will henceforth serve as a refuge for self-discovery, a community where we support each other on the path to a more empowered life. As we open our doors, we invite you to embrace the beauty within and without. May this space become your sanctuary—a wellspring of inspiration and motivation. So, here's to a journey of self-love, unwavering confidence, and endless growth!'

Alessia concluded her address, raising her glass of sparkling white wine in a toast.

A tremor of emotion ran through her voice as she concluded by thanking her mother, the woman who had shaped her into the compassionate soul she was today. Her gratitude extended to her steadfast patients, whose trust was the bedrock of her practice. Then, her gaze met mine for a fleeting moment as she thanked us, her friends, for urging her to evolve—not just as a professional, but into a stronger, more fulfilled version of herself.

Bravo, my remarkable friend! Alessia's inspiring speech cast an ethereal energy that made her stand out as the shiniest figure in the oatmeal-hued room. As she spoke, I couldn't help but notice her captivating presence, commanding attention with each word. The room seemed to glow with her enthusiasm, and she truly became the focal point of the event. Capturing her gaze twice, I noticed her eyes lingered on Giorgio's brother during the course of her address. His name was George. Yes, really. The coincidence of their names was not lost on me, and I couldn't help but chuckle at the thought of meeting the parents who thought that was the right choice.

The two stylish Italian men were like a pair of finely crafted dark leather shoes made in Italy, alike in every aspect. Their Italian flair was obvious in every detail. It felt as if Dolce & Gabbana themselves had stepped into the clinic. With the arrival of these Italian guests, the beauty clinic was poised to open its doors to not only a new era of aesthetic excellence, but also to the charm and charisma the two of them brought along, making it an evening destined to be remembered.

A few minutes after her address concluded, Alessia found her way to my side to grab my elbow, rather firmly.

'Hold the phone,' she whispered, half out of breath.

'Have you ever seen a man in a bathrobe look this good?'

George was basically channelling a Greek god in that white linen number he showed up in. It draped over his broad shoulders like a toga fit for Mount Olympus, showcasing enough muscle to make a personal trainer weep tears of joy. And don't even get me started on those white linen trousers peeking out from underneath. It was like he ripped a page straight out of a Hamptons lifestyle magazine.

But here's the thing about George: he wasn't just about the designer labels (although those Loro Piana loafers were definitely shoegasm-worthy). There was a relaxed confidence radiating from him, evidenced by the fact that he could rock a bathrobe to a gala and still be the most stylish guy in the room. And those eyes! Deep brown pools that sparkled with mischief and genuine kindness. But it was the smile, that million-dollar smile with teeth whiter than my Manolos after a fresh cleaning, that truly stole the show. Seriously, everyone in the room practically did a double take. And he knew how to use that smile.

Both Giorgio and George were working their magic. Frankly, with those smiles, they could sell ice cubes in a blizzard. They effortlessly quipped with guests they had never met before, welcoming humorous banter about themselves with equal enthusiasm (because a confident man can laugh at himself). It wasn't just about the clinic launch anymore—it was a full-blown fiesta of friendship, laughter, and newfound connections.

The room buzzed with the energy of Alessia's design genius, but these two guys added a whole other layer of fabulousness. It was the perfect blend—Alessia's vision sparkling like a million diamonds, and these two Italian imports bringing irresistible charm. Talk about a night to remember!

Alessia's vision of her clinic was nothing short of revolutionary. Far more than slapping on a mud mask and taking some medicines. We're talking about a consultation that goes beyond the usual 'What moisturiser do you use?' routine. Think lifestyle audits, dietary confessions, even a little love life chit-chat—nothing is off-limits! With patients' permission, of course, Alessia whips out all the high-tech toys—full body scans, skin and blood tests, allergy and food sensitivity assessments. Thanks to cutting-edge tech, the patient is in and out in 30 minutes, with a detailed report landing in your inbox within two days.

Then comes the magic. Alessia takes everything you shared in the consultation and combines it with those in-depth test results to craft a personalised beauty roadmap just for you. We're talking bespoke diet and exercise plans, customised skincare routines packed with the right products, and even targeted treatments to address any specific concerns. And if something falls outside Alessia's expertise? She'll connect the patient with the top specialists in the branch. This wasn't just about the in-clinic experience. Alessia was all about holistic wellness, inside and out. Think post-workout fuel delivered straight to the door—healthy, delicious, and portion-controlled, because nobody wants to do math after a killer spin class. And for the truly dedicated, there's even a weekly meal prep service, all prepped and packaged for easy reheating. Forget takeout menus and greasy spoons—this was going to be gourmet wellness!

And let's not forget the social side! Alessia's idea wasn't just about transforming the body; it was about transforming one's social circle, too. Picture yoga sessions with your besties, meditation circles fueled by lavender lattes (because self-care is all about the little luxuries), or maybe a high-energy barre class followed by a champagne brunch. Alessia even dreamed of hosting interest groups—think healthy breakfast potlucks, artisanal bread tastings, or even fancy cocktail parties with a healthy twist! Basically, a country club for the wellness-obsessed, a place to focus on yourself while having a little fun in the process.

And can we talk about community? Signing up at Alessia's clinic with Sophia by my side felt like signing up for a whole new chapter in our lives—a transformative path towards a healthier, happier, and undeniably more radiant us. We raised our glasses, toasting to the emergence of our best selves, stronger, fitter, and ready to conquer the world (or at least, that killer spin class). Alessia's clinic was about to become our new favourite hangout—and it was going to be fabulous!

Alessia's strong, independent personality was evident in her ability to stand on that stage by herself and command an entire room, yet she also enjoyed flirting and attention. While she didn't need a man to complete her life, the idea of companionship seemed to hold some appeal for her. Watching Alessia and George together, I couldn't help but notice the intriguing dynamic they shared—a dynamic that seemed poised to evolve beyond friendship. And fast. Both possessed strong personalities, but George, with his gentlemanly demeanour, seemed to intuitively understand the delicate balance of their interactions.

As they interacted, it was clear he had mastered the art of balance—knowing just when to let Alessia shine and assert herself while also stepping in to take charge at the perfect moments. Two unique personalities, each a star in their own right, but somehow complementing each other like a sequined clutch and a pair of statement Manolo Blahniks. Perfect on their own, but undeniably fabulous together. The chemistry between them was sizzling hotter than a Rome sidewalk in July. The clinic launch might have been Alessia's big moment, but there was a definite possibility of a new chapter unfolding in her personal life. Buckle up, dear reader—this could be a love story for the ages!

Giorgio, although he had booked a hotel for the trip, ended up spending the night at Sophia's. She later told me she felt more at ease being on her own turf, which gave her the confidence to dig into Giorgio's past and ask him what really happened about his most recent long-term relationship.

The early years saw the couple facing the profound sorrow of losing a child, an event that cast a lingering shadow on their attempts to start their family. Despite this tragedy, they remained together for twenty years. However, instead of growing closer, each passing day seemed to widen the emotional gap between them. The once-intimate connection faded, leaving them as strangers in the latter years of their relationship. Her newfound interest in hunting, bringing the scent of blood into their home and culminating in the preparation of the creatures she hunted for dinner, became a source of discomfort and disgust for Giorgio. Love gave way to repulsion, yet he stayed, feeling a sense of obligation. He was convinced that she needed him.

It was his girlfriend who, sensing his silent sacrifice, ultimately gave him the freedom he longed for by saying, 'You can go; I don't need you.'

With those words, he silently departed, leaving behind a relationship that had become a mere shell of what it once was. When Sophia inquired about Giorgio's fidelity during their time together, his unspoken admission hinted at the complexities of his experiences. Cheating, usually deemed as the worst transgression in matters of relationships, found an unexpected approval from Sophia in Giorgio's situation. It was a revelation that surprised even her, as she had never imagined there would be circumstances where she would condone such behaviour.

Perhaps it was the depth of his struggles, the resilience he displayed despite having his heart broken in more ways than one, or the growing affection she felt for him that influenced her perspective. It might have also been the distance from the situation, as neither she nor her friends were directly impacted by the infidelity, making it somewhat easier for her to come to terms with it. Giorgio's life had been marked by hardships and setbacks, yet he projected an outward happiness that belied his inner turmoil. His ability to maintain a facade of contentment despite facing profound personal challenges spoke volumes about his character and ability to endure. Despite facing the devastating loss of two unborn babies and the love of his life, Giorgio found a way to persevere and maintain a semblance of happiness. Amidst the tangled threads of his past relationships, one constant source of unwavering love and support remained: his tight-knit family. His parents, stationed in London, and his brother, who had built a life in Paris, served as steadfast pillars in his life. And then there was his niece, Aya.

George, Giorgio's brother, met a Parisian lawyer a lifetime ago, and it was instant amore. He followed her across the Atlantic, built a life in France, and together they had a daughter —his mini-me, as he proudly referred to her. Giorgio, too, adored his niece. Through the various stages of her life, from tender moments of holding her as a baby to witnessing her metamorphosis into a young girl and engaging in discussions about global issues as a teenager, Aya was his rock through it all.

Sophia contemplated the possibility of Giorgio still wanting children, and she acknowledged that it might normally have been an opportune moment to broach the subject. However, she hesitated and refrained from asking the question. Though there was uncertainty about whether Giorgio would ever want to have a child of his own, Sophia felt a strange sense of commitment to him, mentally declaring that she wouldn't mind if his response turned out to be negative. She wasn't ready to give up on him, regardless of his stance on starting a family.

The brothers seemed really close to each other, and it also appeared that my closest friends really liked those Italian Englishmen. I found it funny that my friends were now starting long-distance relationships, considering for the first time in a while, I was no longer involved with men across borders.

The following evening, the quartet hit up our favourite Japanese spot for a double date. Meanwhile, I was going on my first date with The Surgeon.

CHAPTER FIFTEEN

Once again, I was hurling myself down the stairs in my trusty Saint Laurents keeping up with my chaotic love life. Forget Cinderella's glass slipper—these beauties hugged my feet like a good friend. Comfy, stylish, and the perfect complement to my hard-earned tan. I still didn't know exactly where we were going, but my Nuits were coming along for the fabulous ride.

It's going to be a great night, I thought to myself.

There he was, The Surgeon, practically posing against his cherry red convertible, the top down like a metaphor for the loosening of his usual uptight demeanour. Gone were the starched suits, replaced by light beige pants that seemed to hold the warmth of the fading evening light. A hint of tan stood out on his neck and face, a souvenir from leisurely afternoons (at the golf course, most likely), adding a touch of outdoorsy ruggedness to his usual city polish.

Of course, the man couldn't resist his crisp white shirt. I also distinctly remember his choice of white sneakers, a selection that, in my humble opinion, should have been replaced with loafers. Nevertheless, even the most discerning among us occasionally make decisions that diverge from perfection. But leaning there, bathed in the golden hour sun, he somehow pulled it off.

The Surgeon, the epitome of refined masculinity, had embraced a laid-back cool that mirrored the balmy autumn evening. It felt like a season of change, a season of possibilities. With deliberate slowness, he opened the door. Gallant, sure, though with the car's low profile and my 120mm heels, a simple hop would have sufficed. I slid in, clutching my Serpenti clutch, and took a deep breath as I gazed up at the wide-open celestial expanse above. It felt like all the stars were aligned, literally and metaphorically. The Surgeon had a way of making the mundane feel magical, and that evening, under the autumn sky, was no exception. It was the first time he asked me out. A seemingly small step for a man but an undeniably significant leap for The Surgeon.

As he skillfully manoeuvred the vintage car through the city lights, my mind raced a million miles an hour. Where was he taking me? Was it going to be different this time? Would I still be so drawn to him if his personality was going to be completely different? With a quick glance in my direction, his eyes sparkled like the skyscrapers reflecting in the windshield.

The vehicle purred to a halt outside a chic restaurant, and with a gentlemanly nod to the valet, he signalled a moment of privacy for us. Between the embrace of the worn leather seats and the gentle hum of the engine, a new chapter in our story was about to begin. It was the perfect setting for something unexpected, something... exciting.

He reached for my hand, his touch sending an instant shiver down my spine. Then, with a flourish worthy of a magic show, he unveiled a crimson box with a gleaming gold edge. The iconic Red Box. Hello, heart attack! The cool leather on my legs sent goosebumps dancing across my skin as I sat forward, but it was the anticipation that truly set me ablaze.

His eyes met mine, a silent conversation being exchanged between us. No cheesy theatrics, no bent knee - this was so him, a dash of old-world elegance with a healthy dose of mystery. And let's be honest, a girl could never resist a little Cartier magic.

'Open it,' he instructed.

My hands trembled, searching for the small metal button to unlock the box.

'Go on, open it. It's not a ring,' he reassured me.

I felt relief. Mingled with a touch of… disappointment.

'But it does pose a question,' he added. 'Would you move in with me?'

He wasn't a man of many words, and I, at that moment, needed only to use one: 'Yes.'

With steady hands, exhibiting true surgical precision, he helped me slip on the bracelet. To me, it wasn't just any bracelet: it was a symbol of something bigger, something that sent butterflies fluttering in my stomach. In my head, I could already picture it sparkling on my newly redecorated nightstand —our nightstand. Our bedroom.

'If you want a happy ending, that depends, of course, on where you stop your story,' wrote the legendary screenwriter Orson Welles. Every story is but a segment, a fragment in time. Where it starts and where it stops, the storyteller holds the pen to define.

The Author

Emilija Pavlovikj, born in 1990 in Skopje, Macedonia, currently resides in Munich, Germany, with her family of four. *Stories from the Shoe Store: Little Black Dress and Big Expectations* marks Emilija's second novel in the engaging Stories from the Shoe Store series. Collaborating with American editor Madison Gile, Emilija proves to be passionate about bringing her unique perspective and creative storytelling to life.

Printed in Poland
by Amazon Fulfillment
Poland Sp. z o.o., Wrocław